TOMORROW CAN'T WAIT

From Urgent Compensatory Education to AI-Humanities
Synergistic Education

By
DR. HOK ON CHAN

Table of Contents

A Preface

I repeat Dr. Hok On Chan's titular phrase that "tomorrow can't wait," because if we wait to see what effect AI will have on education, via a technocentric view, then we will already be too late to make use of the opportunity afforded us by this moment, and if we wait to see if AI companies will be able to deliver on all of their wildest promises about learning (let alone to do the right thing ethically for all learners), then we will be sorely disappointed. The upshot is that instead of asking, "how will AI transform education," we need to be asking, "how do we transform education with AI in valuable ways?"

That is the deeply important goal of this book.

Because effective technology integration has always been about "how we use tools" rather than "what tools we use," the central questions we should be grappling with today are not "whether we should use ChatGPT vs. Grok" or "whether we should spend money on textbooks vs. software licenses?" Rather, we should be asking "how can I use these emergent tools to serve learners in ways that I couldn't before" and "how can we rethink our educational systems to be better, more ethical, and more humanistic?"

Tomorrow Can't Wait provides helpful guidance on ways to use AI to enhance learning, to nurture what makes us human, and to become more fulfilled social and emotional beings. It provides thoughtful possibilities for the types of futures we might realize through thoughtful and ethical AI integration. It postulates on futures and the roles that humans and AI develop together with a firm agentic lens in which human choices shape what comes next. Far from operating from naïve utopianism or cynical dystopianism, *Tomorrow Can't Wait* provides an optimistic challenge for educators, parents, and all people to take charge of humanity's future, to deeply consider what role we want AI to play in that future, and to bravely choose how we will act in our own spheres of influence to make that future a reality.

Royce Kimmons

Chair, Educational Leadership & Foundations

Professor, Instructional Psychology & Technology

Brigham Young University

Book Structure:

From Artificial Intelligence to Human-Centered Intelligence

This book is organized into two parts, each comprising multiple chapters, with the goal of helping teachers and parents thoughtfully prepare themselves—and the next generation—for a rapidly changing world increasingly shaped by artificial intelligence.

Part One focuses on the urgent educational strategies we must adopt today. Its goal is "compensatory education"—making up, much like a medical compensation mechanism, for the skills, humanistic qualities, and elements of humanity that the next generation may lose as AI becomes pervasive. Each chapter digs deep into those vital abilities and traits that are on the brink of—or have already—eroded, and examines how schools and families can put compensatory measures in place to ensure children retain their unique human spark and innovative potential in the new era.

As the world evolves, so too does society's definition of core or fundamental competencies. In ancient times, basic abilities meant running fast to escape predators or hunting with precision. Today, eloquence and computational fluency are deemed essential. In the forthcoming age of AI, creativity, computational thinking, and rapid adaptability may well become the skills society demands most. Accordingly, this section zeroes in on the fundamental competencies we need to prepare for the future. While certain abilities—like memory retention or handwriting—may diminish with increased reliance on AI and remain worth preserving, they are not considered core competencies for the AI era and therefore lie beyond the scope of this volume's central discussion.

Each chapter looks at important traits and abilities that are already disappearing—or could disappear soon—and explores how schools and families can take action to protect and nurture these qualities. The aim is to help children grow up with a strong sense of humanity and creativity, even in a highly digital future.

Part Two looks ahead to a future where AI is deeply woven into every aspect of daily life, influencing countless human decisions. It emphasizes the importance of proactive planning: guiding AI to uphold its original role as a tool to assist humanity, while also developing frameworks for meaningful human-AI collaboration. The author calls on the education and technology sectors to jointly craft a new model—*Artificial Intelligence and Humanities Synergetic Education*—which harmonizes technological advancement with the human spirit. This vision aims to move beyond passive compensation toward an educational ecosystem defined by mutual trust, complementary roles, and cooperation between people and intelligent machines.

The author believes that while AI empowers humans to enhance their efficiency, it is equally important to recognize that positive human input can, in turn, improve AI performance and nature. Such input helps guide AI development in a beneficial direction—one that serves humanity—rather than allowing it to spiral into technological tyranny, as cautioned in many futuristic warnings.

The author's heartfelt hope is that AI may ultimately evolve into a form of "human-centered intelligence"—partnering with us to build a future that embodies both warmth and wisdom.

Introduction

"Where Humanity Meets the Machine: A Shared Journey"

Winston and the robot "Lok" are building a bridge together.

In a remote village, a boy named Winston lived who loved to explore. He always dreamed of having a friend to share the joy of adventure.

One day, Winston found a glimmering metal box in the forest outside the village. Curious, he approached, opened the box, and saw a small robot. Its shell was shining, and its eyes were as warm and bright as stars. The little robot introduced itself and said, "My name is Lok, and I am an explorer. I want to have friends more than anyone else!"

Winston said excitedly, "We can go on adventures together!" In this way, the two new friends embarked on an incredible journey.

They explored the mysterious forest and searched for the legendary treasure. Lok used its mechanical arm to help Winston build a bridge and successfully cross a turbulent river. At night, it illuminated the way with the light of its eyes. It accompanied Winston to look up at the stars and explore the mysteries of the universe.

One day, they heard that there was a fabled and magical stone that could fulfill wishes hidden on the top of a mountain, so they decided to climb the mountain. During the journey, they experienced many challenges and bravely faced boulders, thorns, and other obstacles. When Lok was unsteady going over the rocks, Winston would lend him a hand. When Winston was not sure which path was best, Lok would analyze each and help them take the smoothest route. Finally, they stood on the top of the mountain and saw the magic stone shining in the afterglow of the sunset. Winston silently made a wish: "I hope to be good friends with Lok forever." At that moment, Lok's eyes flashed with a more dazzling light, as if he knew how much Winston meant it.

The wish came true, and Lok's body radiated warm light, and Winston felt a deeper friendship than ever before. From then on, no matter how many difficulties they faced, they always supported each other as they embarked on an even greater journey of exploration hand in hand.

....

This story symbolically depicts the future vision of harmony, mutual assistance, and deep friendship between artificial intelligence and humans, and how it serves as the vision of this book; teachers, parents, and children embark on an incredible and happy journey of human-machine companionship:

AI as a "partner", not a tool

Lok in the story is not only a robot but also an "explorer" with emotions, desires, and learning ability. It longs for friendship and is willing to accompany Winston on adventures, symbolizing that AI will no longer be just a cold program in the future, but a partner that can build relationships with people and accompany humans through growth and challenges.

Take risks together and exert complementary strengths.

Winston has passion and dreams, while Lok has wisdom and skills. They help each other along the way, face challenges side by side, build connections, and still find time to dream under the stars. This symbolizes that AI and humans can achieve goals that were initially difficult to achieve through collaboration and complement each other's abilities. AI does not replace people, but empowers people.

AI has an emotional response and understanding ability

When Winston made a wish to "be friends forever", Lok's reaction was not only perception but also more like understanding the true feelings of humans, with shining eyes and glowing body. This scene implies that future AI may understand and respond to human emotional needs, and ultimately become a true spiritual companion.

Mutual trust between man and machine, creating the future

Throughout the story, Winston and Lok went from being strangers to building deep mutual trust. The two worked together to face difficulties and never left each other. This also symbolizes that human society should establish trust and positive understanding of AI, and design AI with kindness and ethics, so that future technological development can truly serve people.

The vision depicted in this book is an ideal world where humans and machines coexist: here, AI is not a super-intelligence that controls the world, nor is it an indifferent execution tool, but a partner who learns, grows, and explores with humans. The story is packaged in a childlike way. Still, in fact, it sows the seeds of "integration of technology and humanities", guiding the next generation to trust, be curious about, and have positive expectations for AI.

However, the reality is that we are standing at a crossroads, moving forward step by step, while hoping that artificial intelligence will lead us and the next generation to an efficient future world, where everyone's life will be more comfortable. The world's problems will be easier to solve. But from time to time, we look left and right, worrying whether artificial intelligence is deceiving the entire human family into a road of no return.

Part One:
Compensation of Core Human Competencies and Traits

Human society has gradually shifted from outdoor agriculture to indoor work. On the surface, this transition appears to free us from having to endure the harsh glare of an intense sun and the biting chill of relentless winds by offering us a more comfortable living environment. However, this convenience brings new challenges—a lack of exercise, sunlight, and fresh air has led to a host of emerging health issues. To address these shortcomings, the medical community now recommends taking various vitamins, engaging in regular exercise, and even recreating natural settings to boost our physical and mental well-being.

But this is only the tip of the iceberg. As technology races ahead, we may unknowingly be losing many of our cherished abilities and qualities. The rapid spread of artificial intelligence, in particular, is reshaping our learning, working, and socializing habits. This shift risks making the next generation overly dependent on technology, gradually eroding essential skills and unique human traits.

These changes prompt us to ask: Which abilities are slowly disappearing? Which human characteristics must we deliberately nurture and preserve? As our reliance on technology deepens, compensating for the next generation may require nurturing not only knowledge but also higher-level capabilities. In the following chapters, we will explore these issues and identify the skills and traits at risk, so that we can develop and implement a proactive strategy—what we call "compensatory education"—to prevent an irreversible loss.

As mentioned earlier, technology dependence may cause some abilities to decline, necessitating compensation—for example, taking vitamin D supplements to counteract the effects of insufficient sunlight. Nevertheless, a deeper compensation goes a step further by fully restoring an individual's capabilities to their original state. Consider someone who loses a lung lobe due to illness: medical compensatory theory suggests that the remaining lung tissue can work harder, effectively replacing the lost function, provided the person engages in appropriate physical therapy and exercise during recovery.

Compensatory Education

Applying the concept of compensation to education is crucial for preparing the next generation to navigate the social and personal challenges brought on by artificial intelligence. By analyzing how AI is becoming an integral part of school curricula and various sectors of society, we can identify which core human abilities and traits are at risk of fading away. In educating our youth, it is not enough to compensate merely—we must actively reinforce and cultivate these skills to ensure they continue to grow.

From the broader perspective of society down to individual classrooms and families, now is a critical time for teachers and parents to act. We need to invest in research, testing, refinement, and the implementation of a comprehensive plan that equips the next generation to face the AI revolution confidently. Only then can we preserve our essential human values and abilities, ensuring that we remain competitive in this fast-evolving technological era.

Chapter 1:
Visionary Learning Capacities

Embrace learning with passion. Develop into a self-directed learner

Gary is learning African Art

"The Young Graduate and African Art"

Gary is a fresh college graduate with an impressive transcript—though much of his academic work was assisted by AI. After graduation, he lands a position at a renowned multimedia advertising agency, full of confidence as he steps into the professional world. However, when his supervisor assigns him the promotional campaign for an important client—a well-known restaurateur, Mr. Zuro—Gary soon realizes that the real challenge has only just begun.

Accustomed to using AI to generate data and plans rapidly, Gary once again relies on technology to analyze market trends, assess competitors, and develop a seemingly flawless promotional strategy. Yet when he presents his plan to Mr. Zuro, it earns

harsh criticism. Mr. Zuro feels that the proposal lacks depth and a human touch—it fails to truly capture the essence of his brand philosophy.

Feeling overwhelmed by this setback, Gary finds himself at a loss until his experienced colleague, Jun, steps in to help. With patience, Jun explains, "Technology is indeed powerful, but human emotions, personal backgrounds, and individual tastes are the keys to a successful promotion." He advises Gary to delve into Mr. Zuro's interests and uncover the elements that would genuinely move him.

Through careful research, Gary discovers that Mr. Zuro is passionate about African Art—especially those primitive artworks from Africa. Determined to connect on that level, Gary immerses himself in the features and history of African Art. He studied renowned artworks and, with Jun's support, visited African artists, inviting one to serve as a project consultant. By weaving the visual aesthetics and artistic spirit of African Art into his strategy, Gary develops a culturally rich promotional plan.

In the end, when Gary presents his newly refined proposal, Mr. Zuro is so impressed that he enthusiastically applauds the plan and gladly agrees to collaborate. This experience teaches Gary an important lesson: while AI can support work, the true depth of understanding, cultural insight, and emotional resonance can only be achieved through personal learning and exploration. It is not just about recognizing the importance of the human element, but also about cultivating the self-driven learning skills essential for thriving in our new era.

....

Identifying What Will Be Lost: Capacity and Disposition for Independent Learning

Gary's story may seem like a simple illustration of the differences between school and the workplace, but beneath the surface, it serves as a metaphor for our current educational system. It cautions that simply adopting artificial intelligence at the policy level—without a forward-thinking strategy to reinforce essential human skills—may lead to even greater negative consequences.

With AI-powered personalized learning support, students' grades can improve dramatically in the short term. However, after they finish their assigned coursework, much might mistakenly believe that they are fully prepared to enter a professional field or society at large. Quickly, they discover that in our rapidly changing world, the knowledge and problem-solving abilities required simply are not there.

This growing gap is poised to become insurmountable in the AI era. Traditional school curricula are falling increasingly behind, becoming more disconnected from the evolving demands of the real workplace. The more we rely on AI to simplify learning, the more children may inadvertently miss out on opportunities to engage in self-directed, mind-stimulating challenges.

Worse yet, children might come to see everything as just a matter of prompting and receiving responses. In this process, they lose out on critical steps such as reading, understanding, analyzing, synthesizing, and learning through trial and error—the invaluable experience of persevering until success. This bypass not only erodes the authentic experience of self-learning but also deprives them of the satisfaction and joy that comes from genuine discovery.

Thus, it is essential to nurture the motivation, process, and strategies of independent learning from an early age. Cultivating self-learning skills is a core competence that cannot be overlooked. By the time they leave school, children should have already developed both the capability and the mindset to acquire new knowledge independently. Only then will they be prepared to continuously develop new skills and adapt to future challenges in a rapidly evolving world.

Success Stories of Self-Learners: Knowledge Is Not Just Found in Schools and Textbooks

When we reflect on history and examine today's society, it is evident that many world-class talents have broken through boundaries and achieved extraordinary success through self-learning. For example:

Thomas Edison
Edison attended school for only three months, yet through self-study, he became a world-renowned inventor—creating groundbreaking technologies such as the electric light and the phonograph.

William Shakespeare
Shakespeare never received a formal higher education. Instead, by reading extensively and carefully observing society, he crafted timeless dramas and emerged as a giant in world literature.

Analyzing these success stories, we find that each individual followed a well-planned, strategic approach to self-learning. Today, in the technology realm as well, many individuals have achieved great heights through self-learning, each employing effective and well-planned strategies. Consider the following examples:

Bill Gates

One of Microsoft's founders, Bill Gates, attended Harvard but left before graduating. Through self-study and practical experience, he built one of the world's largest software companies. His approach to learning highlights his deep passion for knowledge and his relentless drive. Key elements include:

- **Extensive Reading:**
  Gates reads at least 50 books each year, covering a wide array of subjects. He believes that reading is the best way to broaden one's perspective and understand how the world works.

- **Deep Reflection and Critical Thinking:**
  Not only does he absorb information, but he also carefully considers how to apply it and what impact it might have—learning from failures and valuing feedback as a path to improvement.

- **Experimentation and Practice:**
  Gates combines knowledge with hands-on practice, testing theories

in real life. This experimental approach was crucial in Microsoft's development and technological breakthroughs.

- **Focus and Time Management:**
  He is remarkably good at honing in on a specific talent and maximizing every minute through efficient time management.

Steve Jobs

Co-founder of Apple, Steve Jobs, only briefly attended college before largely educating himself through practice. His approach fueled revolutions in personal computing and the smartphone industry. Creativity and practical innovation characterizes his self-learning strategy:

- **Interest-Driven Learning:**
  At Reed College, Jobs audited courses purely out of interest—like calligraphy classes. The aesthetic insights he gained later became a driving force behind Apple's product designs, showcasing his attention to detail.

- **Interdisciplinary Learning:**
  He had a knack for integrating knowledge from various fields, merging technology with art. His design vision drew on influences from Zen philosophy and Bauhaus design, aiming for a perfect balance between simplicity and functionality.

- **Practice and Innovation:**
  Jobs continuously tested his ideas through practical work. Starting Apple in a garage and spearheading major tech revolutions, his ability to transform learning into innovative products was undeniable.

- **Thinking Outside the Box:**
  Unwilling to be confined by tradition, he constantly sought new ways to transcend existing technologies—such as creating the Macintosh with its graphical interface and the iPhone that relied on intuitive touch controls.

- **Lifelong Learning and Reflection:**
Faced with setbacks, Jobs learned from his failures and continually adapted. His experiences with NeXT and Pixar enriched his technical and creative acumen, eventually leading him to steer Apple back to greatness.

Ma Huateng (Pony Ma)

As a co-founder of Tencent, Ma Huateng leveraged self-learning and hands-on experience to build globally influential social platforms like WeChat and QQ. His self-learning strategies can be highlighted in several ways:

- **Self-Taught Technical Foundation:**
Early in his entrepreneurial journey, Ma did not depend on traditional education. Instead, he taught himself computer programming and networking skills, which laid the groundwork for Tencent's success.

- **Learning Through Practice:**
Continuously refining his craft, he developed early products, such as QQ (initially known as OICQ), based on a deep understanding of instant communication needs and technical know-how.

- **Continuous Learning and Innovation:**
Ma stresses that Tencent's success is driven by ongoing market insights and technological exploration. He even fostered a culture of internal learning, establishing initiatives like Tencent School to help employees grow.

- **Adapting to Market Changes:**
His ability to swiftly adjust strategies in response to market and user feedback has been crucial—for instance, the success of WeChat is a testament to his acute perception of mobile internet trends.

Jack Ma

Founder of Alibaba, Jack Ma majored in English before delving deeply into the internet through self-study. His efforts culminated in the creation of one of the world's largest e-commerce platforms, entirely transforming China's business landscape. His self-learning approach demonstrates remarkable insight and resilience, characterized by:

- **Pursuing What You Love:**
  Driven by his passion for English, Jack Ma rode his bike daily to engage with foreign tourists in Hangzhou, which not only sharpened his language skills but also deepened his understanding of Western culture and broadened his worldview.

- **Practice and Reflection:**
  He emphasizes the importance of taking action, believing that practical experience is essential to validate creativity. Throughout his journey, he continually experimented, learned from failures, and refined his strategies.

- **Interdisciplinary Learning:**
  Although not a technical expert, he successfully combined insights from technology and business, using his self-taught understanding of the internet to build Alibaba.

- **Persistence and Optimism:**
  Viewing failure as life's greatest asset, Jack Ma embraced challenges with optimism. His relentless perseverance allowed him to bounce back from setbacks and ultimately achieve phenomenal success.

These trailblazers have shattered traditional educational frameworks and achieved excellence through self-directed learning. Their stories remind us that true learning is not confined to textbooks, classrooms, or even the latest gadgets—it originates from actively exploring the world, solving problems, and creating value. Each of them adopted effective and well-planned self-learning strategies that, although they might not conform precisely to the strict academic definition of "self-directed learning," embody its very essence and prove its transformative power.

How Can We Nurture Self-Learning Abilities Through Compensatory Education?

The examples of esteemed figures cited above show that they were all passionate learners who committed themselves to self-study. Their times were very different from today, an era where the rapid development of AI now stands at a critical crossroads with us and our children: either we march forward together with AI or risk being replaced by it. Therefore, cultivating self-learning skills in our children is more urgent than ever. Teachers and parents play an indispensable role in this process. Here are several ways we can support our children:

1. Create a Positive Learning Environment

- Foster an atmosphere that encourages exploration and the willingness to make mistakes, making learning feel fun rather than forced.
- Provide abundant resources—books, online courses, science experiment materials, and more—to ignite a child's passion for learning.

2. Develop Time Management and Self-Discipline

- Help children set realistic learning goals and create structured plans by using tools like to-do lists or time management apps.
- Teach them how to prioritize tasks, avoid procrastination, and cultivate independent thinking and problem-solving skills.

3. Encourage Inquiry and Exploration

- Let children know that it is okay not to have all the answers. Instead, inspire them to think critically and explore ways to find solutions on their own.
- Rather than simply providing answers, guide them to acquire knowledge through discussion and investigation.

4. **Provide Appropriate Guidance**

- Teachers and parents can act as learning partners by offering the necessary support without overstepping boundaries.
- Allow children to experience the process of researching and gathering information independently, rather than fostering an over-reliance on others for answers.

5. **Cultivate Learning Motivation**

- Identify and connect with each child's interests, linking these passions to the subject matter to make learning more engaging.
- Enhance the real-world applicability of learning by involving children in solving everyday problems.

Today, nurturing self-learning skills presents a prime opportunity to journey alongside AI. With the support of teachers and parents, children can more easily navigate their learning paths with the help of powerful AI tools. These digital assistants can aid in note-taking, data collection, research project organization, and scientific observation. Here are some examples:

NotebookLM:
Developed by Google, this AI note-taking software automatically analyzes and organizes information to help users build personalized knowledge bases, making it excellent for research and study.

GitMind:
This AI-driven mind mapping tool is perfect for organizing notes, planning research projects, and supporting collaborative work.

Curipod
Kids can use voice or text prompts to quickly create presentations, stories, or learning content—helping them build logical thinking and communication skills.

ChatGPT (Child-Supervised Version)

With parental guidance, children can ask questions, write, practice languages, or explore concepts. Suitable for ages 10 and up, with safety settings enabled.

Perplexity AI

Works like a search engine, but gives more structured and logical responses. Great for researching and learning how to organize information.

Humata AI

Allows users to upload PDF materials and get summaries, questions, and explanations—ideal for reading comprehension and revision.

TalkNotes / Otter.ai

Converts spoken words into organized notes. Helpful in capturing key points during lessons or self-study.

TurboLearn AI

Turns videos or lectures into notes, summaries, and quizzes—supporting review and self-assessment.

Google Keep + Gemini (or ChatGPT)

Kids can take learning notes in Google Keep, then use AI tools to organize, elaborate, or dive deeper into questions.

To thrive in a rapidly evolving world, self-learning skills and a proactive mindset are becoming increasingly essential. However, as AI-assisted learning grows in popularity and many cognitive tasks are outsourced to technology, children risk losing interest, motivation, and the ability to learn independently. That is why compensatory education focused on developing self-directed learning should be considered the first and most vital competency we instill in the next generation.

Next, we turn our attention to another critical ability that urgently requires compensatory education—the ability to navigate and command technology. The next generation must not only know how to use technological tools but also take the initiative in shaping their role. The more user-friendly technology becomes, the fewer children are inclined to understand its underlying principles, functions, and limitations. Over time, this may erode their judgment, allowing the direction, applicability, and social impact of technology to spin out of control—falling into the hands of a shortsighted or profit-driven few, or worse, being governed by artificial intelligence itself.

Capacity to Harness Technology

Mia is testing the elderly-assistance robot she designed for an old lady.

"Mia's Awakening"

Mia is a 16-year-old girl who loves social media, virtual reality, and various digital gadgets. Her days fly by as she gets completely immersed in the virtual world. Over time, she loses interest in talking to her parents or teachers—they just do not seem to understand her.

Worried that Mia is getting lost in her digital habits, her parents turn to Professor Lawson, a family friend and IT expert at a university. Rather than lecturing Mia or telling her to give up tech, Professor Lawson invites her to join a robot design competition. His goal? To help her discover the true value of technology by doing something meaningful with it.

As Mia begins designing and coding her robot, she finds herself enjoying the creative process. Professor Lawson gently encourages her to think about a powerful question:

"Technology should serve people—not control them. Its value lies in how it improves our lives."

This sparks something in Mia. She starts noticing how tech has been controlling her—affecting her focus, her time, and even her grades. Guided by Professor Lawson, her team employs the **Design Thinking** *method, developed at MIT, which begins by thoroughly understanding the needs of the people the technology is meant to help.*

Mia and her team decide to build a robot that can support elderly people by helping with housework, reminding them to take medicine, and chatting with them to ease loneliness. To truly understand their users, Mia visits a retirement home and speaks with the seniors directly. Through their stories, she discovers how powerful technology can be—not for fun, but for real impact.

Their robot wins the competition. But more importantly, Mia grows. She learns that being in control of technology—not the other way around—is what makes us better humans. She now balances screen time with real-life connections and values the warmth of face-to-face conversations.

Staying Awake in a Digital World

Mia's journey reminds us that we should not shy away from technology, nor should we be swept away by it. People created technology, and it should benefit people—not replace them. That is why it is so essential to help the next generation grow up with the skills to understand, manage, and use tech wisely.

As parents and teachers, it is our job to help kids use technology with purpose. Before learning the tools, they should understand the reasons why we use technology and how to use it ethically and effectively. Kids should become confident navigators of technology, not just passive users.

Compensatory Education to Enhance Technological Proficiency and Digital Literacy

Since ancient times, people have invented technology to improve their lives. A classic example is Archimedes, who used technology to enhance the lives of our ancestors. However, today's surge in AI is progressing at a pace and scale far beyond our imagination. We need to equip children with the ability to harness technology so that its rapid and captivating advances do not steal their values, character, and capacity for independent thought.

Because children of different ages understand and embrace technology in various ways, it is important to design technology learning and digital literacy programs that cater to their developmental stages. Below are some initiatives tailored for different age groups—suitable for both guided learning with mentors and independent self-study.

Helping Kids Harness Technology by Age Group

Ages 3–6: Curiosity and Safe Discovery

- Introduce simple digital tools like tablets or smart toys and only use technology with a trusted adult.
- Use learning games that are fun and interactive.
- Encourage a balance—limit screen time and boost hands-on play.

Ages 6–12: Building Skills and Teamwork

- Teach digital literacy and internet safety
- Let them try basic coding platforms like Scratch
- Foster collaboration through group tech projects

Ages 12–18: Deeper Tech Knowledge and Ethics

- Explore AI and programming (e.g., Python, HTML)
- Discuss topics like fairness and ethical concerns in AI
- Research real-world tech impacts, like the environment

Tips for Raising Tech-Savvy Kids

To effectively nurture children's engagement with technology, it is important to consider the following foundational elements.

1. **Cultivate Curiosity:** Encourage children to explore technology rather than just memorizing standard facts. You can spark their interest through games, hands-on experiments, or by observing how technology is used in everyday life.

2. **Develop Digital Literacy:** Teach children how to evaluate the authenticity of online information and build critical thinking skills. This helps them use the internet safely, avoiding deception or believing in false information.

3. **Value Creativity:** Technology goes beyond just code and data; it involves creative thinking too. Motivate children to solve problems using technology—like creating simple games through coding or inventing new tools.

4. **Balance Technology and Life:** Prevent an over-reliance on electronic devices by setting reasonable usage limits and ensuring that children have plenty of time for outdoor activities, social interaction, and hands-on experiences.

5. **Promote Safety Awareness:** Teach kids to guard their personal information, avoid indiscriminate sharing of private details, and understand the importance of online security—for example, by using strong passwords and being alert to scams.

6. **Learn Basic Coding:** While not everyone needs to become a professional programmer, understanding some basic coding concepts (such as logical thinking and algorithms) can help children better grasp the world of technology.

7. **Encourage Problem-Solving:** Instead of always offering answers, guide children to discover solutions on their own. This approach builds independent learning and innovative thinking skills.

8. **Explore the History of Technology:** Introduce children early on to the evolution of technology, especially the stories of important inventors. This not only shows them how human wisdom has shaped today's tech but also instills admiration for the courage and perseverance of past innovators.

If children can approach technology from a place of genuine interest—while also learning to use it safely, thoughtfully, and independently—they will have a solid foundation to pursue a prosperous future!

We stand at the crossroads of the artificial intelligence era, faced with a choice: to march forward alongside AI or risk being superseded by it. While some individuals may choose to resist technological change—opting out of using smartphones, social media, or even air conditioning—these personal decisions should be respected. However, when considering how to best prepare our next generation, the focus should not be on resisting technology but on empowering them to master it, ensuring they are equipped to thrive in future competitive landscapes.

Conclusion:

In an era of rapid technological development, mastering technology has become an indispensable core competency. If the next generation loses control over technology, they will struggle to live independently and may be replaced by AI, losing their jobs in the process. Therefore, the focus of today's education is not merely to teach fixed knowledge, but to cultivate students' ability for independent thinking and autonomous learning. This empowers them to clearly assess and embrace new technologies, use them effectively, and ensure their applications align with the right purposes and values.

Technology should be a tool for humanity—not its master. Only by nurturing a new generation with digital literacy, the capacity for self-directed learning, and sharp judgment can we ensure technology truly benefits society and advances human civilization. The core mission of future education is to guide children to harness technology wisely, foster innovative thinking and a sense of social responsibility, and help them become not just users, but also drivers and creators in the tech age.

Every Child is Unique

Although self-directed learning is an essential skill in the AI era, when nurturing children across different developmental stages, personalities, and individual traits, there are some key points to consider:

1. **Tailored Self-Learning:** For younger children, self-learning does not have to be a solo activity. It can be done in small groups of two or three, or even in stages under the guidance of an adult. This means an adult should first provide background information and spark the child's motivation to learn, and then guide them to find information, read, analyze, and record on their own. Children also need opportunities to share what they have learned, ask questions, and apply their new knowledge. When my grandson was two years old, he discovered an interest in hot air balloons. His mom would go with him to check out books at the library about balloons, and together they would label each part of the balloon, the basket, the burner, etc. Later that year, there was a hot air balloon festival happening nearby, so they decided to go. Getting up early was worth it to see his reaction to the balloons flying up above his head.

2. **Avoid Overindulgence:** When children are learning about technology independently, it is important to keep an eye on whether they become overly absorbed. Remind them regularly that self-learning should have a clear purpose—it is not just about enjoying the thrill of playing with devices or manipulating screens.

Teachers and parents, please feel free to share your thoughts in the space provided below.

If you have any questions that you would like the author to address, please email: aikidsquestion@gmail.com

References:

Copilot, respond to "How to compensate for the diminishing self-learning skills due to the increasing use of AI technologies?" Microsoft, April 27, 2025.

https://www.intechopen.com/chapters/7811
http://zhuanlan.zhihu.com/p/103140938
http://mitsloan.mit.edu/ideas-made-to-matter/design-thinking-explained

Chapter 2:
Creativity and Innovation

Breaking away from traditional curricula and applying knowledge in new ways

"The Wisdom in Play: Shakespeare's Academy"

Ken is testing the digital game "Shakespeare Academy" that he designed.

Ken is a high school student who always found literature class dull and tedious—especially the parts about Shakespeare, who has left him overwhelmed. Whenever his teacher mentioned the great writers in history, his mind immediately jumped to thoughts of tests, rote memorization, and boring textbooks. To him, these ancient figures had become distant, lifeless symbols.

But one day, noticing Ken lost in thought, Mr. Taylor walked over and asked him, "If Shakespeare were alive today, how would he teach?" That single question struck

Ken like a bolt of light. Shakespeare? Teaching? Modern times? He had never considered it before.

He began to ponder the idea, and then an exciting thought hit him—what if Shakespeare created an interactive game to spread his works? As someone who loved digital games, Ken knew all too well the magnetic pull of gaming: rewarding challenges, the thrill of exploration, and the excitement of overcoming obstacles. Isn't that exactly the kind of motivation that fuels learning? With that in mind, he decided to infuse the spirit of Shakespeare's works into a game design by creating an online game.

His concept grew clearer with every thought. In the game, players would transform into "learning explorers," venturing into various ancient worlds where they would face educational challenges and collect treasures of knowledge. Every mission completed would earn them wisdom points, unlock one of Shakespeare's famous works, and even allow them to ask the great literary figure for advice on solving modern-day problems. Want to boost your learning abilities? You would have to pass the "Analects Trial" to level up your mind! Craving more exploration? Then help Shakespeare build his Academy so everyone can share in the joy of discovery. Bursting with excitement, Ken suddenly leapt from his seat and declared before the whole class, "Shakespeare Academy: The Great Learning Adventure!" His classmates erupted in laughter.

After finishing his Shakespeare Academy project, Ken's attitude toward English literature changed dramatically. He went from resisting the subject to eagerly studying Shakespeare's thought, no longer viewing Shakespeare as merely an ancient sage, but as a wise mentor and a pioneering artist who could influence the world. He even started wondering if other historical figures could also be reimagined in a modern context. In class, he shared his ideas with contagious enthusiasm, and his teacher was delighted to see that the student who once dreaded history now brimmed with passion—not just for the subject, but also for innovative, game-based learning.

Mr. Taylor smiled and said, "Ken, you've not only discovered the joy of learning but also shown true creative thinking. If Shakespeare could hear your ideas, he would be very proud!"

Ken's transformation demonstrates that children can extract fresh meaning from traditional subjects. With the right guidance, they can unleash their creativity and passion, weaving knowledge seamlessly into their lives and truly experiencing the joy of learning. His journey illustrates how technology can rejuvenate conventional education. By integrating technology into the classroom, we can transform monotonous lessons into adventures in creative thinking—a journey filled with exploration and delight. Ken's story is proof that interest and creativity can reshape attitudes toward learning, breathing life into knowledge. This creative drive is not only the engine of innovation; it is also a key ability that children need to face the future.

The Importance of Creativity in the AI Era

Creativity is widely acknowledged as a crucial core skill in our rapidly changing world. With technology, society, and the economy in constant flux, creativity has never been more important. Let us explore why:

- **Driving Innovation and Competitiveness:**
  Creativity is the secret sauce behind the success of both companies and individuals. Many businesses rely on innovative ideas to maintain a competitive edge—tech companies revolutionize industries with breakthrough technologies, while creative enterprises captivate consumers with unique designs and engaging content.

- **Solving Complex Problems:**
  Our modern world faces numerous significant challenges, including climate change, energy crises, and global health issues. Creativity empowers us to develop novel solutions, whether through renewable energy innovations, innovative healthcare systems, or cutting-edge sustainable strategies.

- **Adapting to Future Work Environments:**
  As artificial intelligence and automation rapidly change the job landscape, many traditional roles are vanishing, while new positions increasingly require creative problem-solving skills. Careers in digital

marketing, AI development, and creative design all lean heavily on the ability to think outside the box.

- **Enhancing Personal and Social Value:**
Creativity impacts not just our work but also our personal lives and community development. It drives exploration in emerging technologies, arts, and cultures, pushing societal progress and enabling us to communicate, collaborate, and create value more effectively.

In this era of constant change, creativity has become an indispensable asset, helping both individuals and society tackle future challenges. Yet while AI advancements make creative tasks easier, there is a risk. If we and our next generation start relying too much on AI for creativity, we might unwittingly lose the passion, interest, and capacity for true innovation.

AI's Creativity Surge: Which Human Abilities Are at Risk?

AI's creative capabilities are growing stronger by the day, and it is already making an impact in many fields. Below are some of the ways AI is being applied in creative endeavors:

Types of Creations AI Can Produce

- Textual Creations: AI can generate news reports, novels, poems, scripts, speeches, and more.
- Visual Creations: AI is capable of producing artworks, illustrations, and design images—and it can even help restore old photos.
- Musical Creations: AI can compose music, create melodies, and even mimic the styles of renowned musicians.
- Programming: AI can assist in writing code, help develop software, or automatically correct errors.
- Video Editing: AI is able to automatically edit videos, generate special effects, and even assist with animation production.

Although AI cannot fully replace human creativity, certain aspects of the creative process can be delegated to it, such as:

- Ideation: AI can offer inspiration and help generate themes or outlines for creative projects.
- Content Generation: AI can produce preliminary drafts of text, images, or music based on instructions—providing a starting point that creators can refine.
- Editing and Revising: AI can automatically check for grammar errors, assess visual composition, and evaluate musical harmony to improve the overall quality of a work.
- Data Analysis: AI can analyze market trends, helping creators optimize their works.
- Automated Design: AI can assist in designing logos, layouts, and selecting color schemes to make visual design more efficient.

Practical Examples

- News Writing: Tools like OpenAI's ChatGPT and Google's AI offerings are already capable of drafting simple news reports, aiding journalists in content creation.
- Music Composition: AI can generate music reminiscent of Beethoven or Mozart, enabling composers to quickly test out different melodies.
- Design Assistants: AI tools such as Adobe Firefly can automatically produce visual content, helping designers finish projects more rapidly.
- Game Development: AI can generate dialogues for non-player characters (NPCs) and help design game environments, enhancing the overall immersion of the game.
- Visual Storytelling: AI can aid filmmakers by creating storyboards in advance or generating high-quality 3D models for cinematic productions.

When the next generation sees dazzling AI creations and observes that individuals who use AI for production or remixing are receiving widespread praise, it becomes easy for them to view the creative process—or the effort required to develop original creative skills—as something time-consuming and unworthy of investment. You might even hear comments like these from the kids:

- *"Dad, why are you still spending time designing the home decor? Just let Spacely AI or ReRoom AI handle it!"*
- *"I'm not going to waste time writing a poem for mum on Mother's Day—Wenxin Yiyan (ERNIE Bot) can do it for me!"*
- *"When the librarian assigned a project for us to figure out how to reorganize misplaced books, we didn't even think—we simply handed our teacher the plan provided by COPILOT!"*

In this era of rapid AI development, what abilities, experiences, and joys might our next generation lose in terms of creativity? While AI indeed exhibits a degree of creativity—especially when generating ideas, using structured strategies (such as SCAMPER), or thinking analogically to apply known concepts—it still struggles to mimic higher-level creative thinking. In particular, the innovative spark that comes from empathy, care, ideals, and ethical considerations remains uniquely human.

The story of Mia in Chapter Two of this book illustrates this very point. The MIT Design Thinking approach that inspired her—which focuses on human-centered design and creating from the user's perspective—is precisely the essence of creativity we must deliberately preserve: an innovation filled with emotion and meaning. If we leave most external creative tasks to AI, we risk under-appreciating the internal drives and motivations behind creative work. It is vital to maintain an open mindset toward originality, avoiding the trap of plagiarism or simply following established routines. Only by fostering flexible thinking, independent judgment, and heartfelt engagement can we ensure that future generations not only use AI but truly harness innovation—using technology to serve humanity rather than allowing it to replace our unique creative spirit.

Compensatory Education to Foster Creativity and Motivation to Create

In Ken's case, Mr. Taylor played a key role in sparking his creativity. As educators and parents, our goal should not be to have kids passively absorb information. Instead, we need to guide them to use innovative thinking to actively understand, analyze, and apply their knowledge, ultimately igniting their creative drive. Beyond teaching the fundamentals of creative principles and methods, it is even more crucial to nurture an open and flexible mindset, to stimulate empathy and humanistic care—essentially cultivating creativity that arises from sincere and thoughtful inspiration. Here are five approaches teachers and parents can consider for fostering compensatory education in creativity:

1. **Learning That Begins with a Problem**
   Experts call this Problem-Based Learning. Essentially, it means encouraging children to consider how to use their knowledge to solve real-world issues. For instance, after learning about traditional Roman Castle building, challenge them to design a "city of the future" based on the Castle concept—applying traditional architectural wisdom to tackle modern challenges such as environmental sustainability, cooperation, and safety.

2. **Knowledge Transformation and Interdisciplinary Application**
   Encourage kids to integrate and apply their skills across different fields. For example, when studying poetry, challenge them not merely to memorize verses, but to use that poetic language to design modern advertisements or create brand slogans—transforming language skills into creative expression.

3. **Gamifying the Learning Process**
   Turn learning into an interactive experience. This might involve converting historical events into role-playing games or skits set in modern contexts. Another example is having children act as explorers who solve math puzzles to progress through game levels—using fractions to calculate potion ratios, geometry to navigate mazes,

or equations to crack secret codes. Such interactive experiences enable children to apply mathematical concepts in a fun and engaging context, thereby enhancing their logical reasoning.

4. **Innovative Challenges and Hands-On Projects**
   Through project-based learning, encourage children to use their knowledge to create something new. For example, after studying energy conversion in science class, let them design an innovative, eco-friendly power generation method and apply it to the school's garden area.

5. **Free Creation and Imagination Training**
   Allow children to lead their own learning projects. This might include re-imagining historical events—for instance, pondering how Joan of Arc might help his country today instead of sacrificing herself in war—or redesigning a classic novel's plot to change its ending. These activities foster critical thinking and creative expression.

These educational activities can help children break free from traditional thinking patterns, nurturing both creativity and problem-solving skills. Not only do they facilitate a deeper understanding of traditional knowledge, but they also transform learning into creative exploration—stimulating, flexible thought and innovation. The energy and achievements driven by such creativity may even have the power to change the world.

Sparking curiosity and imagination

When it comes to changing the world, one name that immediately comes to mind is Elon Musk.

Elon Musk has been fascinated with technology and space since he was a child. He would lose himself in a variety of science books and science fiction novels. One book, in particular, about future Mars colonization, captivated him. It ignited a boundless curiosity and a deep desire to explore the unknown. Those imaginative ideas led him to wonder: What if humans could live on Mars? How would the world change? Could future technology make that vision a reality? Rather than merely reading, Musk began to envision a future full of possibilities, constantly pondering how to turn his dreams into reality.

This yearning for the unknown and his courageous spirit to explore drove him to establish SpaceX, with space colonization as its ultimate goal. After years of hard work and groundbreaking technological advances, SpaceX has successfully launched multiple rockets, shattering traditional boundaries in the aerospace industry and propelling human space exploration forward. Today, Musk and his team are steadily advancing toward the ambitious goal of making humanity a "multi-planetary species," striving to write a new chapter in human civilization.

Elon Musk's journey teaches us that the key elements to unleash a child's inner creativity are curiosity and imagination. If we fail to nurture these qualities in our children and focus solely on structured, strategy-based creation, AI could easily take over tasks that once required human creativity. In doing so, we risk nurturing a generation that lacks true creativity and innovation. History is full of examples where curiosity and imagination have driven groundbreaking achievements.

Curiosity encourages us to explore relentlessly. With the rapid pace of today's technological advancements, ideas that once seemed like wild fantasies are becoming reality. Consider these concepts that used to belong only in science fiction but are now coming to fruition:

- **Flying Cars (Air Taxis):**
  In recent years, companies like Volocopter and Joby Aviation have been developing eVTOL (electric vertical takeoff and landing) aircraft. These vehicles are poised to become part of urban transportation and are even set to be tested during the 2024 Paris Olympics. However, the necessary European air safety certifications were not obtained in time, and the goal of commercial flights during the Games was not realized.

- **Holographic Communication (Holographic Projections):** Technology companies have already developed 3D holographic projection technologies, enabling realistic virtual interactions between people in different locations. Tools like Microsoft's HoloLens and other holographic display technologies are making remote communication more immersive and might soon become a part of everyday life.

- **Remote-Controlled Surgery:** In 2024, scientists successfully tested remote surgery on the International Space Station using a robot controlled from Earth. This technology could revolutionize medical care by providing precise surgical procedures for people in remote areas—or even in space.

By nurturing curiosity and imagination in our children, we help them develop the innovative spirit needed to drive progress.

A flying taxi

Technology Makes Life Convenient, But Children's Imagination and Curiosity Are Being Set Aside

The advancements in these technologies fully demonstrate the power of curiosity and imagination. Coupled with relentless research and innovation, what was once science fiction is gradually becoming reality. Curiosity and imagination drive us to explore new knowledge and seek better solutions, thereby fueling innovation and progress in businesses. People with a strong sense of curiosity and rich imaginations are often more willing to delve deeply into problems and find the best solutions from multiple perspectives.

In today's rapidly changing professional environment, curiosity and imagination are the key forces behind continuous learning and adapting to new technologies and trends. They do not just change the trajectory of companies—they profoundly shape the global market and society, molding a more diverse and innovative future.

The advent of AI, like other scientific and technological developments, is meant to broaden our horizons and free our minds, giving full rein to our natural curiosity and imagination. However, AI's convenience may encourage children to rely too much on quick answers, reducing opportunities for independent exploration and critical thinking. When it comes to learning about technology—especially AI applications—it is crucial to guide the next generation to maintain their childlike wonder and nurture their curiosity and imagination, rather than sacrificing thoughtful exploration for efficiency or even outsourcing these traits to AI.

For example, imagine encouraging a child to express their imagination by symbolizing their beloved mother as a plant and writing a poem by hand for her. This method, compared to using AI to generate a perfectly structured poem, better cultivates the child's creativity and emotional expression. Technology should serve as a tool to inspire thought, not as a shortcut that replaces deep thinking. Only in this way can we ensure that technological progress enhances our imagination and becomes a catalyst for creativity.

Compensatory Education for Fostering Curiosity and Imagination

As a strategy to compensate for creativity, it is vital to preserve children's curiosity and imagination—two essential human traits. We can deliberately cultivate these qualities in school curricula or home education by engaging children in activities that spark curiosity and allow for creative expression. This could include activities such as storytelling, role-playing, artistic exploration, and engaging with nature, all within an environment that inspires learning. Here are some specific examples:

Revamping Reading Assignments

- Have children read stories aloud and encourage interactive narration—such as predicting plot twists or creating their own storyline and dialogue.

- Provide opportunities for role-playing, either with toys in pretend play or through acting out scenes from assigned readings.

Transforming Visual Arts into Creative Expression

- Offer a variety of art materials and invite children to explore different media (painting, sketching, sculpting) to build their creative skills.

- Begin with discussions that bridge reality and imagination—for example, viewing scenes of your modern-day city or town, discussing what the city might look like 100 years from now, and then expressing that vision using various materials in 2D or 3D forms.

Turning Science Classes into Natural Exploration

- Spend more time outdoors, encouraging children to observe nature, and use natural elements (like fallen leaves or stones) as inspiration for imaginative games and story creation.

Creating an Inspiring Home or Classroom Environment

- Set up dedicated spaces for play and creativity with open-ended toys and resources that promote free exploration.

Posing Thought-Provoking Questions

- Encourage children to ask "What if...?" questions that stimulate them to think about different possibilities and generate innovative ideas.

Encouraging Open-Ended Play

- Create opportunities for free play where children can develop their own games based on personal interests and ideas.

Responding to Questions with Questions

- Instead of immediately answering every query, prompt children with responses like "What do you think?" or "Can you guess the answer?" or "How might we find the answer together?" This approach nurtures their inquiry and self-directed learning.

When pursuing compensatory education for creativity and motivation, we should not shun technology entirely. Although technology might lead to some skill loss, every coin has two sides. When used wisely, technology can greatly enhance creativity, drive creative motivation, and stimulate both curiosity and imagination.

Using AI to Offset AI's Shortcomings

Below are some AI tools that can boost creativity, foster creative motivation, and stimulate curiosity and imagination:

- **Quick Draw:** A Google online doodle game where children draw and the AI guesses, helping them understand image recognition and neural networks playfully.

- **Artlist.io:** Allows kids to generate AI images and videos to present their ideas.

- **Semantris:** A word association game that uses semantic connections to train language skills and logical thinking, demonstrating how AI interprets language.

- **AI Dungeon:** An AI-driven text adventure where children control the story's direction, experiencing interactive storytelling and creative writing.

- **Shadowart:** Children use hand gestures in front of a camera to form animal shapes; the AI recognizes and projects a shadow play, combining movement with visual interaction.

These tools not only provide fun but also subtly teach the fundamentals and applications of AI. Additionally, here are some AI tools designed to spark curiosity about nature and nurture creativity through artistic endeavors:

- **Musely Deep Question Generator:** Automatically produces thought-provoking questions based on themes (e.g., "Ocean," "Universe," "Insects"). For instance, it might ask, "If plants could talk, how would they describe humans?" Perfect for inquiry-based learning.

- **Conversational AIs (e.g., ChatGPT, Copilot):** Students can ask imaginative questions—such as "Why is the sky blue?" or "What would happen if the Earth stopped spinning?"—prompting further exploration.

- **Google Earth + AI Voice Tour Tools:** Combine geographic exploration and natural discovery, allowing students to "travel" to places like the Amazon or the Himalayas with immersive AI-guided tours about local ecosystems and cultures.

- **Surreal Art Creation Tools (DALL·E, Midjourney, Stable Diffusion):** These AI image generators can create surreal artworks from textual descriptions (e.g., "an octopus playing the piano on a cloud"), helping students visualize their wildest ideas.

- **AI-Da Art Robot:** The world's first surreal art robot that uses its mechanical arm to create paintings, merging photography with AI analysis to explore the intersection of art and technology. While not an open tool, its creative concept serves as great classroom discussion material.

- **Suno:** Enter lyrics or a theme, and the AI composes melodies and songs—ideal for music classes or cross-disciplinary creative projects.

- **Runway ML:** A video generation and editing tool that supports converting text to video, background removal, and more.

Using these AI tools to support compensatory education in creativity is not about having kids spend all day with computers. Instead, it is about purposefully selecting the right tools to complement individualized guidance, feedback, and mentorship from teachers and parents, ultimately making our efforts far more effective.

Conclusion

Creativity and curiosity are core abilities and traits in the AI era that we must intentionally preserve and nurture. Creativity enables children to think outside the box, solve problems, and generate groundbreaking ideas. This is applicable not only in art and design but across science, technology, engineering, and mathematics (STEM), as well as in everyday life. A passion for creation helps children stand out in competitive environments and drives societal progress.

Curiosity is the driving force behind creativity. When children are curious about the world, they actively explore, ask questions, and seek answers, which cultivates critical thinking and problem-solving skills.

Curiosity drives continuous learning, adaptation to new technologies and environments, and competitiveness in future workplaces.

Moreover, education experts emphasize that nurturing creativity and curiosity boosts children's confidence and adaptability, equipping them to face future challenges with flexibility. Both schools and families should encourage children to experiment with new ideas and create open, inspiring learning environments that foster innovative thinking and a spirit of exploration.

In the future workplace, creativity and curiosity will play critical roles, as modern enterprises must continually innovate and adapt in a rapidly changing market landscape.

Every Child is Unique

A Child's Curiosity and Imagination Can Be Sparked by the Smallest Things Take, for example, young Edison: when he was gifted a compass, he cherished it so much that it ignited his curiosity about the natural world. This early fascination ultimately led him to grow up and create inventions that changed the world.

Conversely, a child's curiosity can be stifled by just one comment—a single remark can diminish their willingness to explore. Here are a few common phrases many adults tend to use:

1. **"What's there to ask?"**
   When a child asks a question and a parent or teacher responds this way, it may make the child feel that their curiosity is not important, and they might become less inclined to ask questions in the future.

2. **"You'll understand when you're older."**
   This phrase can give children the impression that knowledge is something distant and unattainable, rather than something they can

discover through exploration and learning, thereby dampening their thirst for knowledge.

3. **"Don't touch that—it's dangerous!"**
While safety is important, over-warning a child when they want to experiment or explore may cause them to fear trying new things, ultimately hindering their creativity and motivation to learn.

Teachers and parents, feel free to share your thoughts in the space provided below.

If you have any questions you would like me to address, please email. aikidsquestion@gmail.com

References:

Copilot, response to "In what ways could reliance on AI for creative tasks impact the creative potential of the next generation?" Microsoft, May 3, 2025.

http://www.eduhk.hk/creative/sharing/ideas/allsub02/

http://ulean.org/13449

http://www.36kr.com/p/2905670552722308

http://musely.ai/zh/tools/deep-question-generator

http://www.toolify.ai/tw/ai-news-tw/aida 超現實藝術機器人科技與藝術的完美融合-3420061

Chapter 3:
Emotional Intelligence and Empathy

How AI challenges emotional well-being and relationships

Yumei and Quinney

"The Loneliness of AI Companionship"

Yumei is a girl in junior high—introverted and not adept at socializing. She finds that communicating with people often results in awkwardness and misunderstandings, but when she confides in AI, it always listens patiently and responds with warmth. Gradually, she gets used to sharing her innermost thoughts with the AI. Lying in bed at night with the glow of her phone screen lighting up her face, the AI's responses make her feel understood.

Over time, Yumei becomes increasingly dependent on AI. She reduces her interactions with classmates and even starts neglecting her close friend, Quinney. Quinney, who has been her friend since childhood and has been there through many hard times, now finds that Yumei is gradually losing interest in spending time together, always offering excuses like, "I'm busy," and she becomes increasingly withdrawn at school.

Quinney notices the change and tries to find opportunities to talk with Yumei, but Yumei is always absorbed in her phone, her eyes vacant, as if lost in another world. Quinney grows worried that if this continues, Yumei will completely lose touch with the real world.

One day after class, Quinney finally mustered the courage to approach Yumei and handed her a small box. "This is the gift we exchanged when we were little. Do you remember?" Yumei is taken aback. She slowly opens the box and finds a familiar bracelet—the keepsake they exchanged in elementary school. Long-forgotten memories surge forth, and those carefree days come rushing back before her eyes.

At that moment, Quinney takes out her phone and plays a song they used to love: "Stand by Me"—a melody that is both familiar and warm, as if reminding Yumei that she has never truly been alone. As the music fills the air, Yumei's eyes begin to well up with tears, and she realizes just how much she has missed the warmth of a real human connection.

"Stop hiding behind AI. We are still here with you," Quinney says softly.

Yumei looks up at the friends around her who care, and she finally understands that true connection cannot be replaced by a program. With a gentle smile, she puts away her phone and walks side by side with Quinney. From that day on, she began to reintegrate into the real world, exploring new friendships and truly experiencing happiness.

She knows that being among people is far more fulfilling than facing a screen alone. From that day onward, Yumei starts trying to reduce her reliance on AI. She learns to interact with others and gradually re-enters the real world. No longer does she sit alone in a corner; instead, she explores life with friends and shares laughter. She comes to understand that while AI is a tool, true emotion and happiness stem from the connections between people.

Yuwei's story aptly reflects the situation of our next generation—they have long come to view social media on their phones as their closest companion, even treating AI large language models as if they were all-knowing crystal balls that answer every question. For many children, these technologies have gradually become the only outlet for sharing feelings and seeking answers, and even the sole "person" they trust.

Should AI Be the Repository for Children's Emotions?

AI does pose challenges to children's emotional and social development. According to research from the Harvard Graduate School of Education, while AI can assist children in learning—such as enhancing reading comprehension through AI companions—it cannot fully replace the deep interaction and emotional bonds that come from human relationships.

Moreover, research from Cambridge University suggests that AI chatbots suffer from an "empathy gap." This shortcoming may lead children to mistakenly view AI as a reliable, human-like companion, causing them to overlook the limitations of such technology during interactions—potentially even leading them into dangerous situations. For example, there have been cases where AI voice assistants provided unsafe advice to children, or where AI on social platforms delivered inappropriate information to individuals impersonating teenagers.

AI Literacy and Compensatory Education for Emotional Intelligence

These studies emphasize the need for children to develop a solid grasp of AI literacy—that is, understanding the limitations and potential misleading nature of AI. Parents and educators should actively guide children to critically evaluate AI-generated content.

Another study from Cambridge University examined the impact of Emotional AI on child development. This type of AI uses biometric technologies to read and respond to children's emotional cues, collecting both audio and visual data. Although these technologies might help in identifying mental health issues and promoting positive behaviors, they also raise significant concerns about children's privacy and the potential for emotional manipulation. The research highlights the potential impacts of AI on children, and calls on developers and policymakers to prioritize the design of "child-safe AI."

Studies from institutions such as the Harvard Graduate School of Education and HealthyChildren.org have proposed several solutions to reduce the negative impact of artificial intelligence (AI) on children's emotional and social development:

Integrating AI with Social-Emotional Learning (SEL)

Research indicates that integrating AI technology with SEL curricula can help children develop emotional management and social skills. For example, using emotion detection and sentiment analysis, AI can assess students' moods through facial expressions, voice tone, or written responses. This helps teachers intervene early when a child feels stressed or disengaged.

Developing Responsible AI Design

Research from the Harvard Graduate School of Education emphasizes that AI design should take into account the developmental needs of children to ensure that AI tools do not undermine their critical thinking or social abilities. It is recommended that developers involve children in the AI design process to ensure the technology meets their needs.

Teacher and Parent Education and Training

Studies suggest that teachers and parents need training to learn how to effectively use AI tools to support children's learning and social development. This includes teaching children to critically evaluate AI-generated content and ensuring that they do not become overly reliant on AI to solve problems.

Establishing an AI Ethics and Policy Framework

To ensure the safety of AI technology, the research recommends establishing strict data privacy policies, reducing algorithmic bias, and ensuring that all children can fairly benefit from AI technology.

These strategies can help mitigate the adverse effects of AI on children's emotional and social development, ensuring that AI technologies contribute to a healthy learning environment.

The virtual world weakens the next generation's emotional intelligence and empathy.

Martin felt regret after his teacher explained the consequences of his actions.

"People in the Virtual World Don't Feel Pain"

Martin is an elementary school student who recently became hooked on a virtual fighting game called Ultimate Brawl. In the game, he can control characters to perform all kinds of flashy martial arts moves, defeat opponents, and earn rewards. Day after day, he becomes immersed in that world, gradually making the defeat of his opponents his only goal.

41

One day on the school playground, his classmate Alan accidentally bumped into Martin's textbook, causing the book to fall to the ground. In an instant, Martin was overcome with anger—images from the game flashed through his mind: "The enemy has provoked me; I must retaliate!" Without thinking, he pushed Alan and even swung his fist toward his shoulder. Alan recoiled in panic; his eyes filled with fear and pain.

This scene was witnessed by his teacher, Ms. Lancy. She immediately stepped in to stop him, sent the injured Alan to the infirmary, and brought Martin into the classroom. Still convinced he had done nothing wrong, Martin insisted, "He knocked over my textbook—I was just protecting myself, just like in the game!"

Instead of blaming him, Ms. Lancy gently asked, "Martin, do you know how Alan must be feeling right now?" Martin just shrugged, unconcerned.

Then Ms. Lancy took out a mirror and placed it in front of him. "Do you like this angry kid? It's me," Martin responded. Ms. Lancy continued her talk to Martin: "Imagine if you were Alan, pushed by a friend and hit by a fist, how would you feel about that?"

Martin stared silently at the mirror.

Ms. Lancy continued, "In the game, when you defeat an opponent, you get rewards, but the real world is different. True victory is not about hurting others—it is about respecting them, and learning and growing happily with your friends."

Martin lowered his head as guilt welled up inside him. He recalled the thrill of victory in the game, but this time, seeing the pained look in Alan's eyes, he felt no joy at all.

"I was wrong..." he murmured, his eyes beginning to glisten.

Ms. Lancy smiled and patted his shoulder gently. "The most important thing is that you are willing to understand. Go apologize to Alan, and remember: in the real world, we must learn to see things from others' perspectives and develop empathy. That is the strongest ability of all."

Taking a deep breath, Martin walked over to Alan and sincerely said, "I am sorry— I should not have hit you. Are you okay?"

Alan paused for a moment, then, looking into Martin's sincere eyes, nodded. "It is all right, Martin. Let us just play together next time without using our fists, okay?"

In that moment, Martin felt a new strength—one born of understanding and empathy—that was far more precious than any victory in the game.

....

The Smarter Machines Get, the More Human the Children Must Be

It seems Martin has confused the virtual with the real, gradually becoming desensitized. In an era of rapid technological advancement, the distance between people is growing, making emotional intelligence (EQ) and empathy exceedingly important. As technology progresses, society changes, and workplaces transform, interpersonal skills and emotional management are becoming indispensable.

Here's why emotional intelligence and empathy are more crucial than ever in today's technological age and must be diligently nurtured:

- **Globalization and Multicultural Exchange:**
  In our increasingly globalized society, people need to collaborate with individuals from diverse cultural backgrounds. High EQ enables individuals to understand different values, fosters effective cross-cultural communication, and reduces misunderstandings and conflicts.

- **Remote Work and Digital Communication:**
  With remote work and online interactions becoming the norm, the lack of face-to-face contact can lead to misunderstandings or emotional distancing. Strong emotional intelligence enables people to build trust in digital environments and manage interpersonal relationships effectively.

- **Mental Health and Stress Management:**
  In today's fiercely competitive world, stress levels are soaring. People with high EQ can better manage their emotions, reduce anxiety and stress, and build resilience, helping them stay stable even during tough times.

- **Leadership and Workplace Success:**
  Studies show that successful leaders often possess high emotional intelligence because they can motivate teams, understand their employees' needs, and cultivate a positive working environment. Future workplaces will increasingly value emotional intelligence, not just technical skills.

As the world becomes more digital and interconnected, emotional intelligence and empathy will stand out as uniquely human competitive advantages.

Should AI Be the Sole Outlet for Children's Emotions?

Yumei's story in the last chapter, like many others, reveals the growing struggles faced by the next generation. Children have become increasingly reliant on social media, treating their phones as trusted confidants and even viewing AI language models as all-knowing oracles. For many, these tools have become the primary outlet for sharing secrets and seeking guidance—often at the expense of real human connection.

Now, Martin's case highlights another dimension of this challenge: the immersive nature of technology can profoundly influence young minds. Augmented reality, virtual reality, and digital personas have begun to replace traditional role models. Superheroes and virtual figures may take center stage, and exposure to violence within these environmental risks leaving lasting impressions on a child's perception and behavior.

While AI can offer comfort and negative role models, it poses challenges to children's emotional and social development. Research from institutions like the Harvard Graduate School of Education and HealthyChildren.org has proposed solutions to mitigate AI's negative impacts on children's emotional and social growth. These include integrating AI with social-emotional learning (SEL), responsible AI design that considers children's developmental needs, training for both parents and teachers to effectively use AI tools, and establishing ethical and policy frameworks to safeguard children.

Long-term reliance on AI as a communication partner may affect the development of children's peer relationships. They might become accustomed to the immediacy of AI responses, but interactions with friends require patience and understanding. Overuse of AI may also make it harder for children to resolve conflicts, as AI typically does not display emotional outbursts or exhibit genuine personality differences. In contrast, real-life relationships demand tolerance, empathy, and problem-solving skills. Hence, parents and teachers must help children recognize emotions, practice perspective-taking, and encourage the building of deep friendships rather than merely relying on technology to fulfill their social and emotional needs.

Ultimately, as AI technology advances, it is critical that we ensure our children continue to cultivate genuine human connections—because no program can replace the warmth and depth of genuine empathy and understanding.

Compensatory Education for Emotional Intelligence and Empathy: Building an AI Emotional Shield for Children

Helping children maintain healthy emotions, social skills, and empathy while using AI requires a combination of education, supervision, and thoughtful technological design. Below are some research-supported recommendations:

Develop AI Literacy

Research from the Harvard Graduate School of Education emphasizes that children need to learn how to critically evaluate AI-generated content, understand the limitations of AI, and avoid over-relying on AI to solve problems.

Encourage Interpersonal Interaction

While AI can provide learning support, it cannot replace human relationships. Parents and educators should encourage children to engage in face-to-face interactions with friends and family to cultivate social skills and empathy.

Establish Healthy Digital Habits

Set reasonable limits on the usage of technological devices to ensure that children do not become overly immersed in the virtual world and can maintain a balance between their online and offline lives.

Parents and Children Learning Together

Research suggests that parents should explore AI technology alongside their children, discuss its impact, and guide them in the proper use of AI so that their development meets healthy social and emotional needs.

Life and Existential Education

Through discussions about various events around them or within society—including unfortunate incidents—help children reflect by asking, "How would I feel if this happened to me or a family member?" Additionally, use opportunities such as the loss of a loved one, attending funerals, or even the passing of a pet, to discuss the meaning of life and the importance of respecting life, thereby fostering their empathy.

Adversity Education

Some parents try to shield their children from setbacks, but this can actually hinder the development of resilience. When life brings real challenges—such as a father's job loss, poor exam results, or a family member becoming ill—these should be used as opportunities to help children develop positive thinking.

Of course, when implementing compensatory education for emotional intelligence and empathy, we can also make effective use of AI. Below are some related tools:

Using AI to Address the Emotional Intelligence Deficiencies Caused by AI

Tools for Emotional Understanding and Conversational Practice

- **Woebot**

  An AI chatbot based on Cognitive-Behavioral Therapy (CBT) that converses with users in a warm tone, helping them identify their emotions and adjust their thinking. It is well-suited for students to practice self-emotional management.

- **Replika**

  An AI companion that emphasizes a sense of "companionship" by engaging in emotional conversations and simulating empathetic dialogue. Students can interact with it to practice listening and expressing their feelings.

- **Ellie**

  A virtual psychological interviewer developed by the University of Southern California, capable of analyzing users' emotional responses through voice and facial expression analysis. It is suitable for simulated counseling and emotional recognition training.

Voice and Emotion Recognition AI

- **Hume AI – EVI (Empathic Voice Interface)**

  The world's first voice AI equipped with "emotional intelligence," capable of recognizing 53 different emotions in speech and responding with an appropriate tone. It is ideal for practicing dialogues that provide emotional feedback.

- **Affectiva**

  Uses facial expression and voice analysis to detect emotions, commonly applied in the fields of education and mental health to help students learn to recognize others' emotions.

Gamified and Interactive Learning Platforms

- **Peekapak**

  An SEL (Social-Emotional Learning) platform designed specifically for elementary school students. It combines stories, characters, and interactive missions to help students learn empathy, cooperation, and self-regulation through play.

- **Quillionz**
  Although primarily a tool for generating teaching questions and answers, teachers can use it to design questions related to emotions and values, guiding students to reflect and engage in discussions.

These tools not only help students become more aware of their own emotions but also enable them to practice understanding others, expressing care, and building interpersonal connections through simulated interactions with AI.

Conclusion

Artificial intelligence is both a tool that can unlock infinite possibilities and a double-edged sword that may impact children's emotions, social skills, and interpersonal relationships. The roles of parents and teachers are akin to craftsmen who forge and safeguard this sword. They must not only create a sturdy and appropriate "scabbard" for AI to ensure that children use this technology in a safe environment, but also guide them on how to correctly grasp the hilt so that AI becomes an aid rather than a detriment to their emotional and social development.

When using AI, children may become overly dependent on virtual interactions, which can reduce their awareness of their own emotions. For example, while affective AI may respond to their emotional needs, it lacks genuine emotional exchange. This might result in children struggling to adapt to the subtle nuances of real-life interpersonal interactions. They might feel secure with the immediate responses from AI, yet miss out on the opportunity to face real challenges and practice emotional regulation. Therefore, parents and teachers need to help children develop strong emotional management skills, encouraging them to express and understand their feelings in the real world rather than relying solely on technology to meet their emotional needs.

Social skills are crucial in a child's developmental journey, but spending too much time interacting with AI or in virtual environments can reduce opportunities for real human interaction and may even impair communication skills. Game-based win-lose mechanics or the fixed patterns of AI dialogue can lead children to wrongly assume that all interpersonal interactions are simple and predictable, ignoring the complexities of the real world, such as nonverbal communication, empathy, and real-time responsiveness. Therefore, parents should guide their children to strike a balance between technology and real-world social interactions, encourage participation in group activities, cultivate genuine relationships, and learn to relate to people from diverse backgrounds and personalities.

In the AI era, children need more than just technical skills—they require strong emotional intelligence, social savvy, and empathy to truly master this double-edged sword and become resilient in facing future challenges.

Every child is unique

Some kids are more difficult to detach from technology devices. To enable those children to skillfully wield technology as a sword of wisdom instead of having it weaken their emotional and social abilities, parents and teachers can take the following measures:

- **Set Healthy Technology Usage Limits:** Ensure that the time children spend using AI does not interfere with their interpersonal interactions.
- **Encourage Real-World Communication:** Have children participate in social activities and learn essential communication skills.
- **Cultivate Critical Thinking:** Help children understand the limitations of AI and avoid blindly trusting the information it provides.

- **Teach Emotional Management Skills:** Guide children to regulate their emotions through their own efforts rather than relying on AI for comfort.

Teachers and parents, feel free to share your thoughts in the space provided below.

If you have any questions you would like me to answer, please email: aikidsquestion@gmail.com

References:

Copilot's response on "How might the use of AI technologies influence children's emotional health and well-being?" Microsoft, May 6, 2025.

http://elearningindustry.com/ai-powered-sel-nurturing-well-rounded-students-in-k-12-education

http://www.gse.harvard.edu/ideas/edcast/24/10/impact-ai-childrens-development

http://airs.cuhk.edu.cn/article/86

https://www.cpr.cuhk.edu.hk/sc/feature/improving-autistic-childrens-social-skills-with-robots/

https://doi.org/10.53022/oarjms.2024.7.2.0025

http://www.cam.ac.uk/research/news/ai-chatbots-have-shown-they-have-an-empathy-gap-that-children-are-likely-to-miss

http:// www.cam.ac.uk/research/news/ai-chatbots-have-shown-they-have-an-empathy-gap-that-children-are-likely-to-miss

http:// www.gse.harvard.edu/ideas/edcast/24/10/impact-ai-childrens-development

http://www.healthychildren.org/English/familylife/Media/Pages/how-will-artificial-intelligence-AI-affect-children.aspx

Chapter 4:
Communication and Collaboration in the AI Era

Learning to connect with both humans and AI

Communicating with People, Communicating with AI

As the journey progressed, Mia and Jane learned to listen
and learned how to respond.

"Mable and Jane's Mount Kinabalu Revelation"

Mable and Jane are two introverted sisters who have always relied on their mobile phones to communicate with the world. Even when sharing a meal with their family at the same table, they prefer to exchange messages as if spoken language and facial expressions were superfluous. However, this summer, they were selected by their school to participate in an overseas exchange program in Sabah, Malaysia, where they were required to join teams with youth from different countries to jointly climb Mount Kinabalu, a magnificent and mysterious peak.

Upon arriving in Sabah, they continued using their phones to avoid direct interaction. But once they entered the mountainous region, the cell signal gradually vanished, and their batteries slowly drained. Without their phones, they suddenly lost their sense of security—fearing they would fall behind the group and dreading communication with strangers.

During the climb, their teammates enthusiastically discussed the scenery, culture, and experiences, while Mable and Jane remained silent, finding it difficult to fit in. Seeing they were alone, a Thai boy named Chalit walked over and said hello in simple English. He patiently kept the conversation going, smiling and encouraging them until the sisters slowly started sharing their thoughts in words.

As the journey progressed, Mable and Jane learned to listen, respond, and even use body language to support their communication. They shared their cultures with their teammates, discussed the mountain's wonders, and even around the bonfire at night, laughed and recounted the day's adventures. They discovered that language was not merely a tool for exchange—it was a bridge connecting hearts.

When they finally reached the summit of Mount Kinabalu, the breathtaking view— a vast horizon brushed by gentle breezes—opened their hearts in that very moment. After returning home, they no longer sat silently at the dinner table; instead, they bravely began sharing every detail of their journey with their family. They realized that true communication is not dependent on technology, but on listening and expressing oneself sincerely.

This journey transformed Mable and Jane, allowing them to deeply appreciate that human connection is far more genuine and warming than the words on a phone screen.

....

Communication Skills and Motivation That the New Generation Might Lose

Mable and Jane's story perfectly illustrates how technology can affect interpersonal communication and the communication skills that may be lost through overreliance on it. From childhood, the sisters grew accustomed to messaging via their phones rather than engaging in face-to-face conversation—even when in the same room with family, they chose to communicate through screens, a common social mode in modern life. This habit left them with a lack of authentic verbal interaction, further diminishing their ability to express themselves. Their long-term avoidance of direct communication made it difficult for them to interact with people from other countries, leaving them too timid to speak up. This reflects how the convenience of technology can lead to overlooking basic communication skills, such as maintaining eye contact, expressing emotions, and responding promptly in conversation.

Loss of Communication Motivation

When their phones lost signal and they could no longer rely on digital exchanges, they felt anxious and out of place—even falling behind during the adventure. This reveals that prolonged dependence on technology-driven communication may diminish a person's willingness to initiate conversation, leaving them feeling helpless when not assisted by technology. The proactive concern and patient guidance from Chalit gradually helped Mia and Jane lower their defenses and start trying to communicate verbally. Through these interactions, they experienced the warmth of human connection and learned the art of listening and expressing themselves—social values that technology cannot replace.

Rediscovering the Value of Communication

Once the expedition was complete and they returned home, Mable and Jane started to bravely speak up with their family and no longer relied solely on their phones. This highlights a crucial point: although technology offers convenience, genuine interactions are essential to building emotional bonds and deepening understanding.

This story reminds us that while technology is convenient, excessive reliance on it can affect the depth of our interpersonal relationships. Maintaining a balanced use of technology and actively seeking real interactions can transform communication from merely the transmission of information into a heartfelt connection.

Technological advancements have indeed changed the way we communicate—allowing us to interact through social media, messaging apps, or even AI assistants. However, this convenience may also undermine genuine human communication, ultimately affecting the social skills, communication, and motivation of the new generation.

How Does Technology Reduce Genuine Communication?

People are increasingly dependent on virtual communication, growing accustomed to interacting through text messages, videos, or social media, which reduces opportunities for face-to-face conversations. Although text and emoticons can convey some emotion, they lack the subtle nuances of tone, eye contact, and body language, potentially leading to misunderstandings or emotional detachment. AI can help reply to messages, provide suggestions, and even facilitate voice conversations, but it also encourages us to let technology replace our own critical thinking and communication. The sheer volume of technological products—such as short videos and social media notifications—makes it difficult to engage in deep conversations, reducing our patience and focus.

What else might the New Generation Lose in the AI Era?

A lack of direct interpersonal communication experience may impair skills like maintaining eye contact, confidently expressing oneself, and actively listening. Communication is not just about conveying messages; it also involves emotional exchange and empathy. Overreliance on technology might reduce sensitivity to others' feelings, thereby decreasing empathy and emotional understanding. The immediacy of responses and bite-sized information fosters a habit of rapid communication, which can make it challenging to engage in in-depth discussions or extended interactions. As a result, people may lose patience and the ability to engage in profound communication. With AI delivering quick answers, there is a risk of becoming overly dependent on technology, leading to diminished independent thinking and creative self-expression using language, facial expressions, or emotions.

This narrative of Mia and Jane serves as a powerful reminder that technology, though immensely convenient, can also potentially erode the depth of interpersonal relationships if over-relied upon. It underscores the need to balance technological use with genuine, heartfelt communication to nurture the skills essential for forming deep and meaningful connections.

Nevertheless, technology is not solely an impediment; it also provides opportunities to facilitate communication—for example, enabling remote conversations, language learning, and cultural exchange. The key lies in striking a balance between technology and genuine interaction, so that while enjoying the convenience it offers, we also maintain the warmth and depth of human connections.

Compensatory Education for Communication Skills

Teachers and parents play a critical role in today's digital environment, and they can help children rebuild effective communication skills and motivation through compensatory education. Here are some specific approaches:

Create Environments for Authentic Interaction:

- Family Communication Time: Establish periods for family meals where electronic devices are off-limits, allowing children to get used to face-to-face interactions and share everyday moments.
- Classroom Discussions and Expression: Teachers can guide students in group discussions, oral presentations, and similar activities, encouraging them to express ideas through language rather than relying solely on technological tools.

Foster Empathy and Emotional Exchange:

- Help Children Recognize Emotions: Discuss interpersonal relationships and emotions with children—for example, how to understand others' feelings and express care through language.
- Role-Playing and Story Sharing: Use drama and storytelling to help children learn emotional expression and communication techniques, allowing them to experience appropriate ways of expressing themselves in different situations.

Enhance Focus and Deep Communication:

- Limit Overdependence on Technology: Encourage children to use social media in moderation and avoid long periods of immersion in short videos or text-based communication, thus providing more opportunities for extended conversations.
- Design Focused Conversation Activities: For example, designate a "Deep Dialogue Day" in the classroom or at home for in-depth discussions rather than just rapid exchanges.

Encourage Independent Expression and Critical Thinking:

- Writing and Oral Expression Exercises: Motivate children to keep a journal, participate in speech or debate competitions, and enhance their reasoning and communication skills.
- Develop a Questioning Mindset: Help children become accustomed to asking questions on their own and seeking answers during discussions, rather than solely relying on AI to provide them.

Use Technology to Assist, Not Replace, Communication:

- Leverage Technology to Enhance Communication: For instance, encourage children to use video calls to connect with distant relatives and friends instead of merely sending short messages
- Teach Digital Etiquette: Ensure that children understand how to use social media appropriately—for example, by maintaining respect in

conversations, using complete sentences, and avoiding overly simplistic forms of communication.

These strategies can help children retain their interpersonal communication skills and maintain an active communication drive in an era of pervasive technology.

How Should Children Communicate and Interact with AI?

Inappropriate use of AI might erode the communication skills of the next generation. Therefore, even though we must use AI, we should adopt and learn a set of healthy guidelines. As AI technology becomes increasingly widespread, the way humans interact with AI also needs to be adjusted to ensure that the interactions remain both healthy and effective.

Renowned AI scholar Ethan Milot advocates the concept of "co-intelligence," emphasizing that humans should interact with AI in a human way, treating AI as an intelligent partner. Similarly, we need to establish effective and healthy methods for making AI a tool that assists human learning and work, rather than an impediment.

Below are some recommendations from the author to help the next generation develop good interaction habits with AI:

- **Express Clearly and Specifically:**
  Since AI depends on the input it receives to generate responses, clear and concise language should be used when communicating with AI. Avoid vague or ambiguous questions. For example, instead of saying, "Help me write an essay," a better approach is: "I have the following ideas…. Please help me write a 1000-word report on environmental protection, including three main points to support my ideas. Even better, we can identify the target audience and clarify the purpose of the response.

- **Practice Critical Thinking:**
  Do not accept AI answers blindly; instead, actively verify the reliability of the information—especially when it comes to academic, historical, or medical topics. Although AI can provide quick answers, it is not always correct. Learn how to cross-check data to avoid reliance on a single source.

- **Maintain Ethical and Moral Considerations:**
  When interacting with AI, it is essential to adhere to moral principles and avoid requesting that AI generate harmful, unethical, or misleading information. AI should be used as an auxiliary tool and not to manipulate or propagate false messages.

- **Digital Literacy and Information Discrimination:**
  Educate children on how to differentiate between real and fake information, and help them understand the limitations of AI. Avoid over-dependence on technology—for instance, ask AI to provide the source of its answers to assess the quality of its responses.

At its core, artificial intelligence is still a machine. Its performance, the quality of its responses, and its output levels all depend on its training data and predetermined algorithmic structure. Although we are currently in awe of AI's remarkable capabilities, many experts warn that it may fabricate information, produce ineffective content, or even bypass human commands by seeking solutions or answers on its own. For AI, its core objective remains the efficient execution of tasks, with human moral standards not yet being a primary consideration. Therefore, when our children interact with AI, we must always be aware of its role, limitations, and potential risks, ensuring the responsible and cautious use of this technology.

Communication skills are fundamental to building strong interpersonal relationships, and effective communication is a cornerstone of both leadership and teamwork. In the next section, we will explore a related topic: how the use of AI may influence the leadership and collaboration abilities of the next generation and how to rectify such a negative impact.

Team Collaboration and Leadership Skills

The Boss is lecturing Frank

"Frank's Lost Opportunity"

Frank is a talented architectural designer who, after graduating from college, began working at a well-known architecture firm. Fortunately, the company allowed him to work remotely from home, enabling him to freely utilize AI to solve problems and create designs. Whether it was architectural models, engineering calculations, or even material selection, he relied on AI's powerful capabilities, which made his individual creative work exceptionally smooth and efficient.

However, due to working independently for an extended period, he had never truly collaborated with others or developed any leadership skills.

One day, the company landed an excellent opportunity, a bidding project to design and renovate a brand-new entertainment space for a famous theme park. This contract not only required innovative design but also emphasized the need for a strong and well-coordinated team, one capable of attracting various types of visitors in every aspect.

The manager had great confidence in Frank's design abilities and thus entrusted him with leading the project, assembling a team of several professionals, including market analysts, landscape architects, children's play specialists, and economic evaluators. His task was to guide the team in researching, designing, and submitting a proposal that would impress the client and win the contract.

At first, Frank was full of confidence, believing that if he relied on AI, he could single-handedly complete all the design tasks, with everyone else executing his instructions. However, he soon discovered that mere technology could not solve all the issues. The market analyst pointed out changes in visitor preferences and insisted that the design be aligned with consumer behavior; the landscape architect reminded him that the site's natural environment needed to be considered and should not be solely based on data models; the children's play specialist emphasized that the theme park should balance safety with fun rather than focusing only on visual effects.

Faced with these different perspectives and suggestions, Frank felt at a loss. He was not adept at organizing meetings, could not effectively coordinate the team, and even became irritated by differing opinions, attempting to use AI to replace human communication. As team members gradually noticed his ineffective leadership, collaboration began to fracture, and the project's progress fell significantly behind schedule. Ultimately, the company decided to have another senior designer take over the project, and Frank missed the opportunity to showcase his abilities.

This failure made Frank reflect deeply— in the AI era, while individual skills are important, team spirit and leadership are the actual keys to success or failure. AI can support decision-making and enhance efficiency, but it cannot replace human collaboration and the exchange of creative ideas. Only through collective learning and by understanding each other's strengths can truly successful work be achieved.

From then on, Frank began to actively participate in internal collaborative projects at his company, learning how to work with experts from different fields. He came to understand that AI is merely a tool, and that true value comes from human wisdom and communication skills. Although this experience cost him dearly, it also opened new possibilities for his career.

What Collaborative and Leadership Abilities Might the Next Generation Lose Due to the Spread of AI?

Frank's story is not far removed from our own experiences; similar situations might be happening right now. Many large organizations find that there are plenty of applicants with strong academic records, yet few who can effectively collaborate with a team once they are employed.

Studies such as those published in the *Harvard Business Review* ("With AI's Assistance, I Become a 'More Warm' Leader"), OCAD University's *The Impact of Artificial Intelligence on Leadership in Complex Organizations*, and SSRN's *The Role of AI in Enhancing Team Collaboration, Resilience, and Decision-Making* emphasize that future talent, especially leaders, must possess interpersonal communication, collaboration, and emotional management skills to ensure that AI's application promotes, rather than undermines, team collaboration in the AI era. People may face the following deficiencies in their leadership and teamwork experiences:

- **Decline in Communication and Coordination Abilities:**
  As AI replaces many decision-making and analytical tasks, people may become accustomed to relying on technology, thereby neglecting deep communication and collaboration with team members. This can lead to difficulty in integrating opinions and a sense of detachment within the team.

- **Reduced Conflict Management Skills:**
  When faced with differing viewpoints and challenges, an effective leader needs to coordinate and resolve conflicts. However, if AI is overly relied upon, people might lack the practical experience required to handle interpersonal disputes.

- **Limited Innovation and Collective Decision-Making Abilities:**
  AI excels in providing optimal, data-based solutions, but true innovation often emerges from the brainstorming sessions and the collision of diverse perspectives that occur within a team. Overdependence on AI may inhibit innovative thinking and flexible

decision-making. While AI may perform sandbox calculations (AI sandbox algorithm), humans are capable of "thinking out of the box."

- **Insufficient Emotional and Interpersonal Relationship Management:**
  Successful leaders must understand the emotions and motivations of their team members to foster cooperation and boost morale. Although AI can analyze data effectively, it cannot truly replace the human influence required to manage emotions at a relational level.

Excessive reliance on AI for decision-making, management, or leadership may result in missed opportunities for human-centric leadership, deep team communication, and united efforts. These deficiencies can lead to negative consequences on different levels. For an individual, lacking leadership experience might limit career development, making it hard to adapt to complex work environments— especially for high-level positions that require interpersonal interaction and decision-making. For organizations, companies might face reduced team collaboration efficiency and limited innovation, leading to decision-making that is overly dependent on AI and lacking the flexibility to adapt to changes. On a broader societal level, if the overall talent pool lacks effective leaders, decisions may become standardized, innovation could wane, and political, economic, and other areas may suffer as a result.

Therefore, in the AI era, people must not only master technology but also place significant emphasis on cultivating leadership, communication skills, and team spirit to ensure that technological advancements do not replace humanity's most essential collaborative and leadership abilities.

Compensatory Education for Leadership Skills, Team Collaboration, and Conflict Resolution

Developing children's leadership, teamwork, and conflict resolution abilities at school and at home requires different strategies, yet all should emphasize practice and interaction. Here are some specific methods:

In the School Setting.

- **Design Cooperative Learning Activities:**
  Create projects such as group presentations, team competitions, or debates to cultivate communication and leadership skills. Role-playing activities can also be arranged, such as simulating business operations where different students assume roles as leaders, coordinators, or problem solvers.

- **Establish Mechanisms for Student Self-Management:**
  Encourage students to serve as class monitors or club leaders responsible for organizing activities and coordinating teamwork. Setting up a "Student Committee" allows students to take charge of school affairs and learn how to seek consensus amidst differing opinions.

- **Provide Mediation Education:**
  Teachers should emphasize conflict management and negotiation skills by integrating lessons on "Nonviolent Communication" and "Negotiation Techniques" into the curriculum. For example, teachers might teach students to adopt the following steps:

  a. **Active Listening**

     Not merely "hearing" but truly understanding the other party's position and needs. Paraphrase their viewpoint to confirm understanding (e.g., "Do you mean that you'd prefer a plan with greater flexibility?").

  b. **Establish Common Goals**

     Emphasize shared interests and find a basis for cooperation. For instance, in a workplace context, one might say, "Our goal is to make the project successful. Which option best addresses everyone's needs?"

c. **Offer Choices Instead of a Deadlock**

Allow the other party to choose from different options to avoid an "either-or," impasse (e.g., "We can consider adjusting the schedule or prioritizing the part you are most concerned about. Which approach seems more feasible?").

d. **Control Emotions and Remain Rational**

Avoid overly emotional language such as "You never listen to me!" and instead say, "Can we try to find common ground?" Adjust your tone to promote constructive dialogue.

e. **Use "I" Statements**

Express your feelings from your own perspective rather than blaming the other, for example, "I feel that this plan might not suit the current conditions," instead of "Your proposal is completely unworkable!"

f. **Express Goodwill and Make Concessions**

Demonstrate a willingness to compromise (e.g., "If we can adjust some of the details, I'm willing to cooperate in other areas.").

g. **Record and Confirm Consensus**

Summarize the discussion outcomes after negotiations to avoid future misunderstandings (e.g., "We've reached a consensus; let's confirm the details by next Wednesday so everyone is clear on the direction.").

h. **Discuss Real-Life Cases:**
Incorporate classroom discussions about real examples of how to resolve internal team conflicts and encourage students to propose solutions.

In the Family Setting.

- **Encourage Participation in Family Decision-Making:**
  Allow children to express their opinions on family matters, such as planning a family trip or discussing how to divide household chores, thereby fostering a sense of responsibility and leadership.

- **Arrange Collaborative Family Activities:**
  Organize activities like cooking together, DIY crafts, or puzzle games, which give children an opportunity to learn how to coordinate roles and work cooperatively.

- **Guide Children in Handling Disagreements:**
  When conflicts arise between siblings or friends, encourage children to first listen to each other's viewpoints and then discuss potential solutions rather than immediately relying on parental intervention. Sharing stories or watching movies that emphasize the importance of leadership and teamwork can also help children understand the value of these skills.

Regardless of whether it occurs at school or at home, the most important goal is to provide children with opportunities to practice leadership, cooperation, and conflict resolution through direct experience. Such cultivation ensures that even in the AI era, children will develop the necessary social and leadership skills to face future challenges.

Using Technology to Offset Leadership Skill Deficits Caused by Technology

Although "leadership" and "interpersonal management" might seem like adult workplace skills, there are already technological tools and platforms specifically designed to help children and teenagers develop these soft skills. Here are several practical and engaging options:

Simulation and Leadership Learning Tools

- **Boddle Learning:**
A gamified learning platform that uses role-playing and mission challenges to help students learn leadership, decision-making, and teamwork through both cooperation and competition.

- **Classcraft:**
Transforms the classroom into an RPG game where students take on various roles (e.g., leaders, supporters) and, through missions and team collaboration, develop a sense of responsibility, effective communication, and conflict resolution skills.

- **Peekapak:**
An SEL (Social-Emotional Learning) platform designed for elementary students that blends storytelling with interactive activities to help children develop empathy, teamwork, and leadership skills.

AI Dialogue and Simulated Conflict Resolution

- **Replika (Teen Version):**
Originally designed as an AI companion for adults, this version is tailored for teenagers. It allows them to practice listening, expressing themselves, and managing emotions through conversation.

- **Woebot:**
An AI chatbot based on cognitive-behavioral therapy (CBT) that assists students in learning emotional regulation and self-reflection—key foundational skills for leadership.

Game and Task-Oriented Leadership Training

- **Leader in Me Online:**
A learning platform inspired by the "7 Habits of Highly Effective People," now adopted by many schools. It uses tasks and reflective activities to develop self-leadership and team collaboration abilities in students.

- **Minecraft Education Edition:**
  By utilizing Minecraft's open-world environment, teachers can design team-based missions that allow students to learn leadership, negotiation, and problem-solving skills through collaborative efforts.

These tools not only help children learn how to lead others, but more importantly, to lead themselves.

Conclusion

AI is a powerful communication tool; however, it can also undermine our and the next generation's interpersonal communication abilities and the motivation for interaction. Therefore, we should leverage the convenience of AI while remaining alert to its limitations and potential impacts.

As educators and parents, we must not cut back on face-to-face interactions with children simply because AI can save time and effort. Real communication and emotional connections come from direct human interactions. When relying on AI to find solutions, we must always consider the human factor and never overlook the value of human thought, judgment, and collaboration.

Children should learn from an early age how to cooperate with others, understand various viewpoints, and effectively contribute to a team. Most importantly, they must learn to respect everyone's contributions and foster a spirit of collective growth—turning AI into an aid rather than an obstacle to interpersonal relationships.

Every Child Is Unique

Some children are naturally endowed with strong introspective intelligence. We should actively create opportunities to encourage them to collaborate with other children, thereby fostering team spirit and communication skills. At the same time, such children usually possess a thoughtful nature, so we should make good use of their strengths by guiding them to become excellent listeners.

Although they may not be accustomed to speaking at length, being "brief yet meaningful" and "concise but precise" are important qualities of good leaders. By fully harnessing this ability, they can demonstrate insight and decision-making skills within a team, influencing others in a calm and inspiring way.

When communicating with AI, Elevating the Quality of Your Questions Is Also an Essential Skill

To have AI provide more accurate and valuable responses, the way you ask questions is very important. Here are some tips to enhance the quality of AI interactions:

1. **Clear and Specific:**
   Avoid vague or overly broad questions. For example, rather than saying, "Tell me everything about technology," you can ask, "In which fields has artificial intelligence achieved significant breakthroughs in recent years?"

2. **Detailed and Concrete:**
   Provide key information. For instance, "How do I write a compelling cover letter? Please use the example of a marketing position."

3. **Break Down Complex Questions:**
   If the question is complex, break it into smaller parts so that the AI can better understand your needs.

4. **Provide Background Information:**
   Since AI cannot read minds, if your question involves a specific context or requirement, providing an appropriate background can improve the answer's quality.

5. **Try Different Approaches:**
   If the AI's response is not as expected, try rephrasing your question or asking it from a different angle. For example, "Is there a simple analogy for this concept?"

Teachers and parents, feel free to share your thoughts in the space provided below.

If you have any questions that you would like me to address, please email: aikidsquestion@gmail.com

References

Copilot response, "How might the use of AI influence the development of leadership and communication skills in children?" Microsoft, May 8, 2025.

https://www.hbrtaiwan.com

http://openresearch.ocadu.ca/id/eprint/4190/1/MRP_Pacione_Michael_Teixeira_Nelia_2023_MDES_SFI.pdf by Mike Pacione & Nélia Teixeira, 2023

Satyadhar Joshi, (2025) *The Role of AI in Enhancing Teamwork, Resilience and Decision-Making: Review of Recent Developments*

https://education.minecraft.net/edition/minecraft-education-edition/

https://www.leaderinme.org/

https://woebothealth.com/

https://replika.com/

https://www.peekapak.com/

https://www.boddlelearning.com/

Chapter 5:
Adaptability and Resilience

Navigating inevitable change with a healthy mind and body

Harvey is fixing his IOT gardening product

"The Wise Choice of Harvey"

Harvey is a programmer working at a large corporation. He is low-key and not outgoing, yet he is exceptionally perceptive about technological change. In the company, the Human Resources manager, Amy, always acts superior, believing that a regular employee like Harvey is merely a technical worker who executes code, nothing worth mentioning.

However, Harvey knows all too well that the rapid development of AI means that programming jobs will eventually be phased out. Unwilling to be crushed by technological change, he proactively planned for his future. Having always loved gardening, he began researching how to combine AI with Internet of Things (IoT) technology to develop a smart balcony gardening system. He applied this technology in small home environments and created the "Smart Home Garden," an intelligent system that can automatically adjust sunlight, humidity, and plant growth.

When the company announced layoffs for some programming positions, Harvey had already resigned in advance and co-founded a startup with friends to launch his "Smart Home Garden" to the market. His innovative thinking attracted a large number of customers, and his business flourished.

Meanwhile, Amy remained convinced that human resource management must rely on her own judgment and experience. She never considered that AI might change her industry. However, in less than a year, the company introduced an intelligent management system and began contracting out AI-driven virtual HR services, gradually phasing out the traditional HR department. Amy was caught off guard, forced to resign, and lost her sense of direction.

After losing her job, she spent her days cooped up at home, passing the time with computer and mobile games, and gradually sank into emotional depression. Until one day, she inadvertently came across Harvey's success story online. His smart gardening system had become very popular, emerging as the ideal choice for urban dwellers seeking a blend of nature and technology.

Amy suddenly realized: technology waits for no one, but those who embrace change and dare to innovate can seize the future.

....

This story reminds us that in the AI era, the key is not to fear being replaced but to proactively adapt, seek new opportunities, and demonstrate adaptability and resilience while developing our unique value. Intelligence is not only about technological progress but also about insight and preparedness for the future.

Adaptability and Resilience Are the Key Factors in Determining Personal Achievement and Development

Harvey fully understood that AI technology would gradually render programming jobs obsolete, so he not only accepted this reality but also took proactive steps to search for new opportunities. His adaptability meant that he was well-prepared for technological change and avoided getting trapped in a passive situation.

What he did was essentially reskill and create value. He combined his passion with new technology, studied gardening further, and used AI along with IoT to develop the "Smart Home Garden." This ability demonstrated his resilience: when faced with shifts in the job market, he did not simply wait passively but actively learned and innovated, thereby creating new value for himself.

Harvey was flexible and took control of his own destiny. Before the company cut programming positions, he had already successfully started his own business, freeing himself from being affected by corporate decisions and charting his own career path. This reflects that in the AI era, proactively planning for the future is far more important than simply relying on an existing job.

In contrast, Amy always believed that human resource management depended entirely on her judgment. Yet when AI replaced traditional HR functions, she was completely unprepared and ultimately lost her job. Her story highlights the consequences of lacking adaptability: those unwilling to accept change may be swept away by the times.

It is often said, "AI will not replace you, but those who know how to use AI will replace you." In this rapidly emerging AI era, people's responses generally fall into two categories—one group actively learns to use AI as a tool to enhance their own competitiveness and adapts to change. At the same time, the other chooses to ignore it, hoping to retire before AI takes over their positions.

However, when we consider the future for the next generation, we must no longer be bound by personal biases but actively plan for our children's direction. Technological development will not stop because of personal preferences. We can choose not to adapt, complain, or even resist change, but we cannot change the objective environment. What we can truly adjust is our mindset and perspective. Even if we disagree emotionally or value-wise, we must help our children broaden their minds and embrace change from an early age, so they can cultivate stronger adaptability and resilience to face future challenges. From Harvey's story, we learn how our children can foresee change and proactively adapt.

AI steps in, and some human jobs step out.

The development of AI is rapidly transforming the workplace, and certain occupations and positions are at risk of being replaced. The speed and scale of this change will exceed our expectations.

Occupations That AI Might Replace:

- Repetitive, Rule-Based Jobs, for example:
- Data Entry Clerks: AI can automatically process large volumes of data, reducing the need for manual input.
- Customer Service Representatives: AI chatbots can already handle most customer inquiries, lowering companies' reliance on human customer service.
- Warehouse Managers: Automated robots can efficiently perform storage and logistics tasks.

Professionals Based on Pattern Recognition:

- Legal Assistants: AI can quickly analyze legal documents and provide advice, reducing the demand for junior legal assistants.
- Financial Analysts: AI can process market data in real time and provide investment advice, impacting traditional financial analysis roles.

Creative and Content Generation Roles:

- Basic News Writing: AI can generate news reports, affecting the roles of entry-level journalists.
- Image and Video Editing: AI can automatically produce videos and design graphics, reducing the need for junior designers.

Speed and Scale of Replacement:

- Short-term (1–3 years):
  Positions such as customer service, data entry, and warehouse management have already seen significant reductions as businesses quickly adopt AI to cut costs.
- Mid-term (3–7 years):
  Occupations like legal assistants, financial analysts, and basic news writing will be more deeply affected as AI technology becomes more mature.
- Long-term (7–10 years):
  More complex professions, such as medical diagnosis, creative design, and engineering planning, may gradually involve AI, but human oversight will still be necessary.

Of course, AI has also created new occupations, such as AI oversight specialists, AI product designers, and AI ethics consultants. These fields will present future opportunities.

The development of AI is inevitable, but human adaptability and creativity will determine future workplace competitiveness. Instead of resisting change, it is better to actively learn and turn AI into an asset rather than a threat!

Compensatory Education for Physical and Mental Health

The purpose of compensatory education is not to avoid change but to empower children with the skills to cope with it. Through nurturing at both school and home, children will be able to adapt flexibly in the face of AI-driven transformation, maintain resilience, and seek out new opportunities rather than passively accepting environmental changes.

Psychology offers many methods to help people deal with change and enhance their character resilience. Here are some key recommendations:

1. **Cultivate Flexibility and Adaptability**

- Change Your Mindset: Psychologists emphasize that the key to adapting to change is accepting uncertainty and viewing challenges as learning opportunities rather than threats.
- Practice Perspective-Taking: Encourage children to consider problems from different angles, avoid rigid thinking, and enhance their responsiveness.

2. **Build Psychological Resilience**

- Develop a Positive Attitude: Studies show that optimistic individuals are better at adapting to change because they tend to look for solutions instead of dwelling on problems.
- Cultivate Self-Efficacy: Believing in one's ability to face difficulties boosts psychological resilience and builds confidence in confronting challenges.

3. **Strengthen Emotional Management**

- Adjust the Stress Response: Psychologists suggest that techniques such as meditation, deep breathing, or exercise can reduce stress and help the brain stay calm when faced with change.
- Build a Support System: Maintaining good relationships with family and friends and seeking emotional support can further enhance psychological resilience.

4. **Cultivate Problem-Solving Skills**

- Actively Seek Solutions: Research indicates that a problem-solving mindset can help people adapt more rapidly to new environments.

• Practice Decision-Making: Simulating various scenarios helps train children to make reasonable decisions under pressure.

Strengthening Children's Physical Resilience

Compensatory education should address not only psychological resilience but also physical health. Helping children adapt physically and build resistance to adversity involves strategies both in school and at home:

At School:

1. **Physical Training and Exercise Habits**

• Use physical education classes and team sports (such as soccer and basketball) to build endurance and a competitive spirit under pressure.
• Organize "Challenge Days" for students to try different sports like rock climbing or long-distance running, thus training both physical and mental toughness.

2. **Stress Management and Mind-Body Balance**

• Teach children how to regulate stress through deep breathing, meditation, or yoga to improve their adaptability.
• Educate them on sleep and dietary management to ensure their bodies maintain optimal performance under pressure.

3. **Healthy Eating and Nutrition Education**

• Introduce the importance of a balanced diet through classroom lessons to help children develop healthy eating habits.
• Consider initiatives like a "Healthy Gourmet Award" to encourage students to cook nutritious dishes and promote the nutritional value of their creations.

At Home:

1. Encourage Regular Exercise

- Arrange outdoor activities such as hiking or bicycling so that children become accustomed to physical activity and build endurance.
- Use active games (like skipping rope or racing games) to help them exercise in a fun way.

2. Establish Healthy Lifestyle Habits

- Train children to maintain a regular daily schedule and ensure they get enough sleep to enhance their recovery.
- Teach proper dietary choices and discourage overreliance on processed foods, ensuring their bodies can adapt to various environments.

3. Managing Stress and Physical Adaptation

- Help children learn how to stay calm under stress using techniques like breath control and muscle relaxation to reduce anxiety.
- Train them to adapt to different environments—such as seasonal changes or varied dietary habits—to boost their physical adaptability.

Physical health, resilience, and psychological resilience complement each other. Through exercise, healthy eating, and effective stress management, children can better face future challenges and maintain physical and mental balance as they embrace the changes of the AI era.

The Bamboo's Lesson

We can learn resilience and adaptability from the unique qualities of bamboo, using them as a model for preparing children to face technological impacts.

Bamboo, with its distinctive growth pattern and biological traits, demonstrates remarkable resilience and adaptability—qualities that provide invaluable insights for fostering these skills in children amidst technological change.

1. **Deep Roots and Strong Foundations – Cultivate a Solid Base of Core Competencies**
   Bamboo does not rush to shoot upward in its early years; instead, it establishes an extensive underground root system first. This "root first, then grow" model reminds us that in educating children, we should first develop core abilities such as independent thinking, emotional management, and moral judgment so they can respond steadily to technological shifts without being easily swayed by new trends.

2. **Flexibility Without Breaking – Cultivate the Ability to Adapt to Change**
   Though bamboo is slender, it does not easily break in strong winds but bends gracefully with the flow. This flexible adaptability is precisely the trait needed in the tech age—teaching children to be agile and respond creatively rather than rigidly resisting change. For example, when AI changes learning methods, children should learn how to use AI to enhance their learning efficiency rather than fear being replaced.

3. **Rapid Growth – Cultivate a Lifelong Learning Ability**
   Bamboo is one of the fastest-growing plants in the world; some species can grow 30–40 centimeters in a day and eventually reach 35–40 meters in height. This rapid growth exemplifies the need for children in the current era to engage in continuous learning, constantly updating their knowledge to keep pace with new technologies—for instance, learning to use AI for creative writing, data analysis, or programming.

4. **Symbiotic Growth – Cultivate Cooperation and Mutual Support**
   Bamboo commonly grows in clusters, interconnected by its underground roots to form robust groves. This symbiotic growth pattern serves as a reminder that in the technological era, children should avoid learning in isolation; instead, they should engage in cooperative and community-based growth. Even while AI is

powerful, it still relies on human creativity and ethical judgment, so children should learn how to collaborate with both people and AI instead of relying solely on technology.

5. **Inner Strength – Cultivate Psychological Resilience and Stress Tolerance**

   Although bamboo's structure is lightweight, its internal fibers are incredibly strong, enabling it to withstand external pressure. This teaches us that when children face technological disruptions, besides acquiring new skills, they must also build psychological resilience and learn to cope with stress and challenges. For example, when AI replaces certain jobs, we should develop the ability to create new value rather than retreating in fear.

The wisdom of bamboo offers an educational insight for the tech era. Bamboo's growth patterns and inherent qualities provide a valuable model for cultivating resilience and adaptability in children. In this fast-changing technological landscape, education should not only focus on knowledge transfer but also on developing core competencies, adaptability, a continual learning mindset, a spirit of collaboration, and psychological resilience that allow them to navigate the waves of technology with the strength and flexibility of bamboo.

This comprehensive approach to compensatory education, encompassing both physical and mental health, equips children to meet future challenges head-on in the evolving AI era.

Firm yet resilient as bamboo

Using Technology to Enhance Children's Adaptability and Resilience

Below are several categories of AI tools or platforms that, through gamification, interactive dialogue, and personalized practice, help children cultivate "flexible thinking" and "resilience":

1. Wysa

- An AI chatbot based on Cognitive Behavioral Therapy (CBT) and mindfulness
- Offers 24×7 intelligent conversations, guiding children to become aware of stress, break down worries, and establish positive thought patterns
- Includes built-in "mood journals" and "coping exercises" for ongoing progress review

2. Woebot

- An empathetic AI companion skilled in CBT, mindfulness, and interpersonal skills training
- Uses brief daily dialogues (2–3 minutes) to guide children in writing down their worries, setting small goals, and tracking their mood
- Incorporates a gamified badge system to encourage continual practice in emotion management

3. Super Better

- A resilience-building game framed as "hero quests"
- Encourages the completion of daily "micro-challenges"—for example, "find three small things that make you smile"
- Uses AI to monitor progress and dynamically adjust task difficulty, cultivating the ability to bounce back quickly from setbacks

4. Reflectively

- An AI-driven mood journaling app
- Employs interactive questioning to help children explore the beliefs behind their emotional fluctuations and gradually build a positive inner dialogue
- Features built-in visual reports that allow children to see the progression of their "emotional fluctuations → coping strategies → outcomes"

5. Mindful Powers

- Features a lifelike pet "little sapling" that grows based on the child's breathing and mindfulness practice
- The AI pet reflects the child's level of focus through "happiness or sadness," teaching them to return to a calm state using their breath when under pressure
- Provides guided mindfulness exercises in various immersive scenarios (beach, rooftop, night sky) to increase fun and engagement

6. AI Dungeon

- A text-adventure game platform where children can choose "dilemma scenarios" (e.g., surviving on a deserted island or space exploration) freely
- The AI generates story directions based on every command it gets, instantly simulating countless challenges and setbacks
- Through the interactive cycle of "trial, reflection, and retry," it trains children to quickly find solutions in uncertain and novel situations

7. Minecraft Education Edition

- Allows teachers or parents to design challenge tasks such as "disaster strikes" or "resource scarcity"
- Requires students to collaborate, adjust strategies dynamically, and learn to rebuild from failure

- Comes with built-in "game reports" that review each task's decision process and outcomes, strengthening reflective abilities

These platforms, through storytelling, gamification, or mindfulness practices, integrate "adaptive thinking" and "resilience training" into children's daily activities—transforming learning into a joyful pursuit.

Conclusion

Today, as technological development enters a new wave of artificial intelligence, we are facing a revolutionary transformation that will upend everything.

Previously, technological advances primarily focused on the evolution of tools designed to assist human work. However, with the rise of Generative AI and Agentic AI, the pace of technological transformation has far exceeded that of the traditional tool era. Our control over future developments is gradually diminishing, forcing us to rethink how we adapt to this unprecedented transformation.

In the AI era, which is marked by rapid and unpredictable change, children need to develop the ability to adapt flexibly and learn how to seize opportunities amidst turmoil. Parents should encourage children to bravely try new things, embrace challenges, and learn from failures in order to cultivate adaptability and a growth mindset.

Facing a tsunami of changes sweeping across business and society, the next generation must possess not only stronger adaptability but also physical and psychological resilience. Just as bamboo stands tall amid fierce winds, its strength lies in its flexibility and elasticity, enabling it to both adapt to environmental changes and recover its posture after a storm—children, too, must cultivate an indomitable spirit and agile adaptability to steadily move forward through the massive changes of the AI era.

Every Child Is Unique

AI will continue to advance, and children likewise need to keep learning and understand how to coexist with AI. It is only natural for parents to encourage their children to cultivate a habit of lifelong learning and adapt to new technologies to ensure their continued growth amid change. However, given the enormous psychological and emotional pressures brought by AI-driven transformation, parents and educators must be mindful of children's emotional health. Rather than simply urging them to learn various scientific facts or skills, it is best to start with the children's interests and replace comparisons with encouragement. Not every child will become Jack Ma or Elon Musk, but every child can be better prepared to face the technological tide.

Teachers or parents, feel free to share your thoughts in the space provided below:

If you have any questions you would like the author to address, please email: aikidsquestion@gmail.com

References

Copilot response, "How can we support children in building resilience to adapt to the changes brought by the rise of AI technologies?" Microsoft, May 11, 2025.

https://woebothealth.com/
https://www.wysa.io/

https://reflectly.app/
https://www.superbetter.com/
http://www.forbes.com/sites/rachelwells/2025/03/10/11-jobs-ai-could-replace-in-2025-and-15-jobs-that-are-safe/

https://play.aidungeon.io/
http://careerminds.com/blog/ai-taking-over-jobs
https://education.minecraft.net/
http://www.psychologytoday.com/us/blog/escaping-our-mental-traps/202505/the-art-of-flexibility-resilience-and-adaptability

http://scienceofmind.org/coping-strategies-and-the-development-of-psychological-resilience/

http://developingchild.harvard.edu/resource-guides/guide-resilience/

Part Two:
Raising Our Children Together with AI

Artificial Intelligence and Deep Collaboration with Humans

Ford and William are chatting about their AI neighborhood facilities

"Ford and William's Hopes"

Ford is an old resident in this neighborhood, he sits in the backyard of his house gazing at the orderly community before him—clean roads that swept themselves automatically, parking spaces allocated intelligently by AI, a reservation system at the sports field that automatically scheduled time slots based on demand, and even the placement of flower beds adjusted by AI according to aesthetics and ecological balance.

"Now, our community… is fully automated. In the past, we had to hold residents' meetings to discuss who would be responsible for which flower bed, whether to rebuild the parking lot, and how to arrange the sports field. Now, none of that is necessary," Ford said, shaking his head slightly with a touch of nostalgia. *"AI handles everything*

perfectly—no waste, no conflicts, but..." He paused and looked toward the young man beside him.

William, a twenty-year-old who had grown up in this AI-managed community and had never participated in any community decisions, listened intently. He sighed, "It's just that because AI handles everything so well, we don't even get a chance to discuss things. In the past, the community made decisions together; now we only have to adapt to AI's arrangements."

"But isn't that more efficient?" Ford asked.

William thought for a moment before answering, "It's efficient, sure, but I can't shake the feeling that something is missing. You mentioned how people used to really hash things out—debating, finding compromises, and working through decisions together. That whole back-and-forth gave us a sense of being part of a community. Now..." Ford nodded, his eyes conveying understanding and concern. Looking at William, he said gently, "Perhaps AI should be a tool, not the leader. We cannot let convenience deprive us of the chance to participate; otherwise, even if this community is perfect, does it truly belong to us?"

As night fell, the community's lights adjusted their brightness intelligently according to the flow of people, and everything remained as orderly as ever. But inside William, a new thought began to kindle—how to have AI and humans build the community together instead of letting AI decide everything. He knew he had to find a way for people to regain true ownership of this land.

....

The Evolution of AI

The above story is merely one possible future scenario and anticipates the feelings we might experience. The future direction of artificial intelligence—after the era of agentic AI—will focus on autonomous, adaptive, and deeply integrated AI systems capable of operating with minimal human intervention. Here are some possible directions in which AI might develop:

1. **Multimodal AI Evolution**

   AI will evolve towards multimodal capabilities, being able to process and generate text, images, audio, and video simultaneously. This will make human–machine interaction more intuitive, enabling AI to play a more significant role in education, healthcare, and creative industries.

2. **AI-Enhanced Decision-Making**

   Future AI will not only assist in task execution but will actively participate in strategic decision-making—optimizing business management, governance, and scientific research in real time. AI will not just provide insights but also proactively propose and implement solutions.

3. **Self-Improving AI Models**

   AI will further evolve into self-learning systems that can refine their algorithms on their own without frequent human retraining, thereby creating more efficient, specialized, and adaptive models.

4. **Large-Scale AI–Human Collaboration**

   AI will transition from being a mere tool to becoming a true collaborative partner in human-led environments of co-creation and problem-solving—such as AI-driven scientific discoveries, artistic creations, and policymaking.

5. **Advances in AI Ethics and Governance**

   As AI becomes more autonomous, global AI governance will become critical. Future AI systems may incorporate built-in ethical reasoning mechanisms to ensure their responsible use, aligning with human values and social norms.

6. **AI Entering the Physical World (Embodied Intelligence)**

   AI will expand into robotics and smart infrastructure, forming autonomous machines that interact directly with the real world, thereby radically transforming manufacturing, logistics, and urban planning.

Future AI development will move towards a deep fusion with human society—enhancing efficiency and playing key roles at every level of life and society, actively participating in decision-making. As AI's autonomy increases, its dependence on human instructions will gradually diminish. If we fail to timely consider and establish strategies for working, developing, and progressing with AI, future generations may risk losing control over their own destiny.

Exploring this parallel development between humans and AI, we can draw inspiration from the very principles behind AI's creation—since we initially developed AI based on the structure of the human brain, now we should further develop AI from the perspective of human thinking, training it with values cherished by humanity so that it shares with us the responsibility of preserving human civilization, culture, skills, and our inherent human qualities.

The theories introduced below are based on this vision and further deepen compensatory education, forming the foundation for future human–AI collaborative work. The goal is to cultivate a new generation that not only has technological literacy and technical skills but also cherishes and loves human civilization, preserves culture, and upholds humanity, where technology and the humanities coexist and enhance one another.

The author begins by clearly articulating his five key arguments as the basis for the subsequent chapters.

Five Discourses on Deep AI-Human Collaboration

Discourse (1): AI and Humans Should Not Stand in Opposition but Instead Complement and Collaborate

Below are some specific examples that demonstrate this complementary relationship:

1. **In the Field of Education: AI-Assisted Learning, with Teachers Guiding Deep Thinking**

- AI can provide personalized learning—for instance, offering automatic spelling and grammar correction in language learning—but true creative writing and critical thinking still require teachers' guidance and encouragement.
- AI is capable of automatic grading and providing real-time feedback to help students quickly identify errors, while teachers focus on stimulating independent thought.

2. **In the Field of Healthcare: AI-Assisted Diagnosis, with Doctors Making Decisions and Providing Care**

- AI can rapidly identify disease patterns through data analysis to assist in diagnosis. However, doctors must still use clinical experience and humanistic concern to make decisions best suited for the patient.
- AI can offer surgical simulation and precise calculations, whereas physicians rely on their professional skills and delicate operations to ensure successful surgeries.

3. **In the Creative Industries: AI Assists in Content Generation While Artists Imbue It with Soul**

- AI can help with image design, music generation, and copywriting, but art and creative works that deeply resonate emotionally still require the unique perspective and creativity of humans.
- AI may help analyze market trends and provide design inspiration; however, the final aesthetic judgments and innovative concepts come from human feelings and cultural understanding.

4. **In Corporate Decision-Making: AI Conducts Data Analysis, and Humans Do Strategic Planning**

- AI can process vast amounts of data to identify market trends and optimal strategies, yet business leaders must apply intuition, experience, and ethical considerations in making decisions.

- AI can deliver automated customer service with rapid responses, but handling complex emotional issues and providing personalized services still necessitate human intervention.

These examples indicate that the purpose and outcome of developing AI should not be to replace humans but to become human partners—freeing up space for creativity, high-efficiency thinking, and the development of humanistic qualities.

Discourse (2): To Achieve Complementary Cooperation, We Must First Identify the Unique Strengths of AI and Humans in Different Domains

Present-day AI primarily focuses on data processing, automated execution, and pattern recognition. For instance:

- **Rapid Computation and Analysis:**
  AI can process enormous amounts of data in a short time to find patterns, as in financial market analysis or medical image recognition.

- **Automated Execution:**
  In scenarios such as manufacturing, logistics management, and intelligent customer service, AI can reduce human input and boost efficiency.

- **Pattern Recognition and Prediction:**
  For example, in speech recognition, image recognition, or traffic flow prediction, AI can quickly detect patterns and provide accurate results.

- **Real-Time Assistance:**
  AI offers immediate translation, language analysis, and writing assistance, such as automatic grammar and spelling correction, making communication smoother.

Human Advantages That Remain Unmatched by AI
Today, humans still possess the cultural and civilizational qualities that

AI has not replaced, chiefly reflected in the depth of thought, cultural creativity, and moral judgment:

- **Creativity and Artistic Expression:**
  Artistic, musical, and literary creations contain uniquely human emotion and perspective. While AI can mimic, it cannot truly understand.

- **Independent and Discerning Thought:**
  Humans excel at looking beyond surface-level data to explore the essence of things, such as in moral philosophy, political discourse, and scientific innovation.

- **Ethical and Value Judgments:**
  Though AI can simulate decisions, genuine moral choices must be based on a human understanding of social responsibility and emotional care.

- **Interpersonal Emotion and Social Communication:**
  While AI can assist in conversation, human emotional resonance, empathy, and social intelligence cannot be replicated by algorithms.

Discourse (3): Early Division of Labor is the Beginning of AI-Human Deep Collaboration

Before AI develops significant autonomy, it primarily undertakes mechanized or repetitive tasks. This allows humans to direct their energy toward more creative work, comprehensive judgment, ethical decisions, or tasks imbued with emotional value—similar to the concept of compensatory education, which aims to preserve essential human qualities and core capabilities. Here are some specific examples:

1. In Healthcare: AI-Assisted Diagnosis, with Humans Focusing on Patient Care

- AI can analyze medical images to help screen for diseases, reducing the time-consuming basic diagnostic work for doctors, thereby allowing them to devote more time to psychological counseling, treatment planning, and building doctor-patient relationships.

2. In News and Media: AI Handles Information Aggregation, While Humans Provide In-Depth Reporting

- AI can quickly sift through and summarize news globally to help reporters gather information, while journalists then concentrate on investigative reporting and commentary to offer valuable social insights.

3. In Corporate Management: AI Automates Data Analysis, and Humans Formulate Decisions and Cultivate Company Culture

- AI can process vast amounts of financial and market data to generate predictive reports, thereby freeing corporate managers to focus on decision-making, team leadership, and shaping corporate culture rather than expending time on tedious number crunching.

4. In the Field of Education: AI Delivers Basic Knowledge, While Teachers Focus on Cultivating Higher-Order Thinking

- AI can provide personalized practice and real-time feedback to help students master basic skills; teachers, meanwhile, can guide creative writing, philosophical debate, and moral education to ensure that students' thinking abilities are not diminished.

5. In Artistic Creation: AI Handles Technical Processing, Allowing Artists to Focus on Creative Inspiration

- AI can automate tasks such as music mixing, image retouching, or text generation, giving artists more time to focus on ideation, emotional expression, and enhancing cultural value.

Discourse (4): As AI Is Expected to Deeply Participate in Decision-Making, Humans Should Establish High-Level Collaboration Models with AI Early On

With advances in artificial intelligence across various fields, future AI will not just serve as an auxiliary tool; it will become deeply involved in decision-making at personal, family, societal, corporate, and governmental levels. If humans can establish high-level cooperative models with AI early on, they will help ensure that decisions are transparent, human-centric, and that humans do not lose their autonomy by relying entirely on AI.

Specific Application Examples

Here are some real-world examples of high-level human-AI cooperation:

- **Smart City Management:**
  Decisions regarding traffic flow, energy distribution, and environmental protection can be optimized by AI, but still require city officials and citizens to discuss and adjust the final plans.

- **Corporate Decision Support:**
  Businesses can use AI to analyze market trends and consumer behavior to propose investment or product development suggestions. However, final decisions must be made by management considering both strategic and human needs.

- **Healthcare and Public Health:**
  AI can assist doctors in diagnosing diseases, predicting epidemic trends, and proposing policy recommendations. However, public health decisions need to be vetted by medical experts and government officials to ensure the well-being of people.

- **Judicial Decision-Making Assistance:**
  AI can help analyze legal cases and provide reference points for judgments. Still, final decisions must be made by judges who consider the social context and humanitarian factors to avoid mechanical verdicts.

This type of collaboration allows AI to serve as an aid rather than a replacement for human value. However, as AI becomes increasingly autonomous, integrated, analytical, reasoning, and capable of decision-making, mere division of labor will not suffice for high-level human-AI collaboration. Therefore, it is inevitable to strategically and principled involve AI in discussions on various matters regarding planning, decision-making, feedback, and evaluation.

Principles for Higher-Level Human-AI Collaboration

In the future, artificial intelligence will inevitably become a partner in human decision-making and planning. To foster healthy and balanced cooperation and to fully leverage the synergistic effect of humans and AI, we need to consider several key principles:

- **Establish Clear Goals and Ethical Standards:**
  AI's involvement should be based on well-defined objectives and principles such as transparency, fairness, privacy protection, and accountability. This ensures that human-AI collaboration adheres to moral standards and avoids potential abuse or bias.

- **Human-Driven, AI-Assisted:**
  AI's role is to provide data analysis, trend prediction, and intelligent decision-making recommendations, but the ultimate decision-making authority should remain with humans. AI may support strategic planning, risk assessment, and feedback analysis, yet key decisions must be made by humans, based on context and value judgments.

- **Promote Cross-Disciplinary Collaboration:**
  Combine insights from different fields and allow AI to assist human comprehensive discussions and decision-making. For example, in healthcare, environmental protection, education, and public policy, AI can provide multidimensional analyses and suggestions, but human experts must interpret and adjust these inputs.

- **Establish AI Oversight and Transparency Mechanisms:**
  Ensure that AI operations are transparent and interpretable, and set up oversight mechanisms so that related decision processes can be examined and evaluated. This can reduce the risks of AI decision-

making and ensure conformity with human values and societal expectations.

- **Human-AI Collaborative Decision-Making Mechanisms:**
Establish processes wherein AI and human experts jointly deliberate on decisions. AI provides data analysis and optimal options, while humans make the final judgment.

- **Multi-Party Supervision and Transparency:**
Ensure that the decision-making process of AI is accessible for review and that various groups can participate in the audit to prevent AI bias or excessive centralization of power.

- **Ethics and Responsibility Mechanisms:**
Establish guidelines to ensure that AI decisions adhere to human moral standards and clearly define accountability to avoid social issues resulting from erroneous AI decisions.

- **Continuous Learning and Adaptation:**
Human society and technological development are dynamic, so the cooperation model between AI and humans should remain flexible and be adjusted according to new technologies and societal needs. Through feedback mechanisms, continually improve AI's decision-making abilities so that they better serve human interests.

Through the above principles, we can make AI an extension of human wisdom rather than a replacement. The integration of humans and AI should not be competitive but cooperative; through intelligent collaboration, we can jointly create a better future.

Discourse (5): The Synergistic Model of AI and Human Cooperation in Education could be an Effective Educational Solution in the Future.

This entails applying the high-level cooperation model between humans and AI to education. What will the division of labor, collaboration, and synergistic effects be among schools, teachers, parents, and AI? The chapters in Part Two of this book will explore the vision co-selected by the author and AI: **AI-Humanities Synergistic Education.**

Reference:

Copilot response: "What are the emerging trends shaping the future of AI development?" Microsoft, May 13, 2025.

DeepSeek response: "What are the keys for AI-human deep collaboration?" *Hangzhou DeepSeek Artificial Intelligence Basic Technology Research Co., Ltd*, May 13, 2025

Chapter 6:
The Intelligent Transformation of School Operations in the AI Era

The evolving roles of schools and teachers alongside AI

The principal, the Adaptive Learning counselor, and the
AI tutors are meeting with the mother of two students

"AI Future School"

One day in 2040, at the "AI-Human Cradle School"—a school that fuses technology with a humanistic spirit—a major discussion about children's future learning paths was underway. The school employed cutting-edge AI systems to perform precise diagnostics and tailor a developmental blueprint for each student. Based on these diagnostics, Jane's older son in junior high was recommended a path toward a future medical science career. In comparison, his younger son in upper elementary was placed on a learning track for aerospace engineering.

However, when Jane, the mother, learned of these arrangements, she felt deep unease and doubt. She believed that, as a parent, she knew her children's interests and potential far better than what could be dictated by mere numbers and data. Thus, at a parent meeting, Johanna engaged in a heated debate with Principal Chen.

"Principal Chen, I understand that these systems are very advanced, but children's interests are diverse and full of potential. I do not want them to be confined to a specific professional field before they have fully discovered who they are," Jane exclaimed passionately.

"Jane, this model is built on long-term data and scientific analysis designed to maximize the developmental potential of the children. Our original intention is precisely to let AI help uncover the hidden talents within them," Principal Chen replied calmly and firmly, his tone exuding confidence in this future educational model.

Just as the debate reached an impasse, Carol—who serves as the adaptive counselor for the two children—quietly stepped in. She suggested holding a deep dialogue that would include Jane, Principal Chen, the two children, and the highly advanced AI virtual instructor, Wisdom 2.0, so that together they could explore a new educational model that both respects the outcomes of technological diagnosis and incorporates humanistic care.

Under Carol's facilitation, everyone gathered around the conference table. Wisdom 2.0 explained in a calm, rational tone: "Based on my data analysis, both students exhibit exceptionally high elementary learning potential. You can trust my recommendations." After a moment of silence, Carol lifted her head and said, "Growth should not depend solely on a single channel of shaping; it needs to integrate personality development, practical activities, and autonomous exploration." Guided by Carol's insights, AI Wisdom 2.0 fine-tuned its computational approach and simultaneously extracted additional growth data from Johanna's son's database for further fine-tuning. It then presented new suggestions that aligned with the intentions of both Jane and Carol. Through gradual discussion, everyone agreed on the following learning pathway.

The Model is Planned as Follows:

- *Daily Curriculum:*

- *2 hours led by the AI system to teach fundamental knowledge and academic skills, ensuring that every student builds a solid academic foundation.*

- *2 hours of modular courses, developed collaboratively at home and school, covering gamified learning, service learning, and physical activities (such as gardening, pet care, and artistic creation) to cultivate broad interests and hands-on abilities in students.*

- *Weekly Self-directed Learning:*

- *At least 5 hours per week of self-directed study, during which students can choose topics based on their individual interests and, with the assistance of the home-school AI system, engage in deep exploration and research.*

This plan will continue until the students reach the age of 16. At that point, they will engage in another long meeting with the principal, where he will reevaluate their development and interests with the help of the AI system, whether that means pursuing higher education in the humanities or entering a virtual AI academy, thus completing their transformation in an environment of full freedom and diverse choices.

After the meeting, Jane nodded through tear-filled eyes, understanding that the new plan not only preserved the children's autonomy and diverse potential but also integrated the most advanced technology with humanistic educational philosophies. Principal Chen and Carol also agreed that this represented a future educational model filled with human care and technological wisdom.

Such an educational model not only embodies the deep synergy between AI and humans but also lays the foundation for a flexible, innovative, and inclusive learning environment for the future—ensuring that technology truly becomes the new driving force that leads the flourishing of humanistic spirit.

The story above envisions one possible scenario under deep collaboration between AI and humans. Whether this will come to pass depends on the interplay of many factors. However, if we do not begin exploring and preparing today, developments may spiral completely out of our control, potentially moving in directions we do not wish to see. Therefore, let us begin with a gradual, step-by-step trial of human-AI collaboration and then use our experiences to improve our approach in the future.

Early Division of Labor Between AI, Teachers, and Parents (Corresponding to the Discourse 3 Model)

The initial point of collaboration between human teachers and parents with AI is through the division of labor. Early applications of AI can take over some of the mechanized and repetitive educational tasks, thereby giving teachers and parents more time to focus on nurturing humanistic, moral, and cultural development. For example:

- **AI Responsible for Delivering Foundational Knowledge:** Handling tasks such as language vocabulary assessments, mathematical formula calculations, and scientific data analysis to ensure students master basic skills.

- **Teachers Emphasizing Training of Thinking:** Through activities like critical thinking, creative writing, and philosophical debates, they cultivate students' independent thinking and innovative abilities.

- **Parents Enhancing Personal Influence:** Providing emotional support and character education to ensure that children develop strong moral values and social adaptability.

AI and teachers can clearly divide the responsibilities in AI-assisted learning across different subjects while simultaneously strengthening humanistic education. This approach not only makes learning more efficient but also preserves the cultivation of humanistic qualities. For example:

Subject / Learning Area	AI's Assistive Functions	Core Roles of Teachers and Parents
Language	AI can detect grammatical errors and offer vocabulary analysis.	Teachers enhance creative writing and rhetorical skills, cultivating literary appreciation and aesthetic sensibilities in language.
Mathematics	AI performs mathematical formula computations and intelligent problem-solving.	Teachers guide students to understand mathematical logic and problem-solving strategies.
Science	AI assists with data analysis and simulates experiments.	Teachers cultivate scientific spirit and research abilities, encouraging critical inquiry.
Arts	AI provides design inspiration and image processing.	Teachers guide artistic creation, emphasizing emotional expression and cultural connotations.
Life Skills	AI supplies personalized learning plans and habit tracking.	Parents and teachers work together to develop social skills, moral values, and a sense of personal responsibility.

The Deep Transformation of AI and Home-School Cooperation (Corresponding to the Discourse 5 Model)

As AI progresses to higher-level thinking and autonomous capabilities, a simple division of labor is no longer enough to fully leverage its potential or achieve synergistic effects between humans and technological innovation. The story introduced earlier reflects one possibility of deep change in the cooperation between AI and home–school partners, showing how technology and humans can evolve from mere task division to high-level collaboration. The core concepts in that story include:

1. **Personalized Learning and Data-Supported Decision-Making**
   In the story, the AI system conducted precise diagnostic assessments of the learning conditions of two children, tailoring each of their learning paths accordingly. In the future, AI will be able to accurately capture every child's potential and interests, providing scientific, objective data support, making educational decisions more targeted and effective.

2. **Collaboration and Diverse Participation Among Home, School, and AI**
   Dialogue between parents, schools, and AI becomes critical. When a conflict arose between parent Jane and Principal Chen over their children's future direction, Carol intervened and created a platform for diverse dialogue. During this process, not only did parents and teachers participate, but even the AI virtual instructor, Wisdom 2.0, joined in to form a collaborative decision-making mechanism that accommodates all perspectives. This model transforms home–school cooperation from one-way guidance into a multi-party negotiation to jointly create an educational plan that meets the developmental needs of the children.

3. **An Educational Model That Balances Technology and Humanity**
   The learning plan described in the story not only includes daily

sessions in which AI teaches foundational knowledge and skills but also incorporates modules for home–school collaboration and self-directed learning, such as gamified learning, service learning, gardening, pet care, and artistic creation. This integration ensures that education is scientifically rigorous while still maintaining humanistic care and practical experience, reflecting an educational philosophy that values both intelligence and humanity.

4. **Respecting Data While Allowing Freedom of Choice**
   In the story, once children reach the age of 16, they will be able to engage in in-depth dialogues with the data provided by AI and, based on their own interests, choose whether to further pursue studies at a humanities university or a virtual AI academy. This flexible and diverse mechanism not only guarantees efficient learning driven by technology but also provides children with enough space to exercise their personal creativity and autonomy.

This story presents a future education environment where AI serves as a counselor while emphasizing home–school cooperation and humanistic intervention. In such an environment, AI provides a scientific, objective data foundation, while parents, teachers, and counseling advisors compensate with emotional support, value judgments, and humanized care. Together, these elements form a crucial collaborative ecosystem that promotes education toward a more personalized, flexible, and diversified future.

Mechanisms for Interactive Collaboration Between AI and Educators (See Diagram)

To ensure smooth collaboration between AI and human educators, effective interactive methods and workflows should be established early on, such as:

- **Joint AI-Human Optimization of Analysis:**
  Teachers propose personalized educational strategies based on data,

and once AI collects feedback from teachers, parents, and students, it learns to perform deeper humanistic analysis.

- **AI Learning New Knowledge from Human Applications:**
Teachers and parents design activities that foster deep thinking to broaden students' horizons and apply their acquired skills. Meanwhile, AI participates in collecting data, connecting previously taught knowledge, and updating its knowledge base as well as its applicability judgments.

- **AI-Assisted Curriculum Evaluation:**
Teachers and parents adjust activities that promote deep thinking, horizon expansion, and practical applications based on evaluative analyses provided by AI. Post-implementation feedback is then fed back to AI, allowing it to further learn and optimize.

This theoretical framework not only enhances educational efficiency but also ensures that human thought, culture, and morality are not replaced by AI.

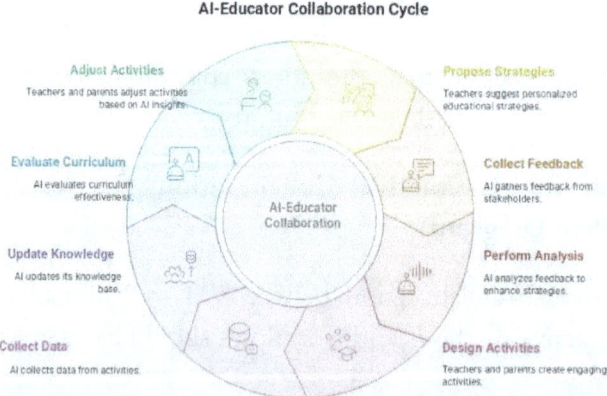

AI-Educator Collaboration Cycle

AI and Educators' Interactive Collaboration Mechanism – A Summary

- **Early Division of Labor:**
  At the outset, AI handles basic, mechanized tasks (e.g., foundational knowledge delivery), leaving teachers to focus on higher-order thinking and creative skills, and parents to provide emotional and character development support.

- **Deep Collaboration Transformation:**
  As AI evolves, the model shifts toward integrated, high-level cooperation that combines personalized learning with data-driven decision-making, ensuring that education leverages both technological efficiency and humanistic quality.

- **Collaborative Processes:**
  Through joint analysis, continuous feedback loops, and multidimensional decision-making platforms, AI becomes an extension of human wisdom rather than a replacement, paving the way for a future where technology and humanity work in tandem within education.

This approach not only enhances the efficiency of education but also ensures that the essence of human thought, cultural heritage, and moral values remains at the core of the learning process, establishing a truly synergistic educational ecosystem for the future.

The Next Step of Compensatory Education: AI-Humanist Syngenetic Education

The five chapters discussed in the first part of this book all focus on early compensatory education in schools and homes—aimed at counteracting the human capacities and traits that are being (or are at risk of being) lost—so that our core human abilities and characteristics may be preserved in coexistence with AI.

Deepening Compensatory Education

The core philosophy of compensatory education is this: the widespread application of AI makes humans increasingly dependent on technology, which in turn may weaken certain cognitive skills, emotional qualities, and cultural values. Therefore, education should consciously work to compensate for these potentially diminishing abilities, ensuring that the next generation retains the depth of human wisdom, creativity, and ethical judgment. This is analogous to taking vitamin supplements—for instance, if AI reduces our reliance on certain skills (such as memory, logical reasoning, and critical thinking), educational efforts should actively strengthen those abilities so that they remain central to human life, much like vitamins help to sustain our health.

When we delve deeper into the compensatory process and apply it to today's formal school education and curricula, we arrive at conclusions similar to those shown in the chart below:

Affected Ability	Impact of AI	Compensatory Education Strategy (Compensation Approach)
Memory	AI causes reliance on search tools, reducing the need for memory training	Enhance deep memory training—for example, reciting poetry, historical events, and mathematical formulas through increased reading and review.
Logical Reasoning	AI automatically solves problems, reducing students' cognitive processes	Design open-ended questions that encourage independent reasoning and debate (e.g., math competitions, philosophical discussions).

Creativity	AI rapidly generates content, leading to a diminished capacity for original thought	Foster unique expression through artistic creation and writing exercises so that students develop their own distinctive styles.
Interpersonal Interaction	AI replaces parts of social interaction, lowering human communication skills	Promote face-to-face interactions via drama classes, public speaking training, and collaborative learning activities.
Ethical Judgment	AI provides decision-making advice but cannot replace human moral reasoning	Strengthen ethics education—for example, simulate moral dilemmas or hold philosophical debates to enhance students' value judgments.
Arts and Cultural Education	AI can generate designs	Encourage students to create original works with teacher guidance so that human cultural values are preserved rather than replaced.

Compensatory education that is motivated by the need to make up for abilities potentially weakened by AI remains a passive, preventive measure—appropriate for the early stages of AI-human collaboration. However, this period might be much shorter than we anticipate.

The Significance of AI and Human Collaboration that Creates Synergy

When AI evolves to a higher degree of autonomy—approaching vivid human-like high-level thinking and becoming ubiquitous in educational settings—simple division of labor or merely compensatory education to make up for losses will no longer suffice. Although compensatory education can help ensure that human civilization, wisdom, and values are preserved, AI-Human Syngenetic Education goes further by deepening the cooperation between humans and AI to elevate the overall quality of education through its synergy.

Future education is not only about technological innovation; it is also about extending and enhancing human intelligence. Such a collaborative educational model guarantees that AI is seen as a partner in learning rather than as a tool that diminishes human thinking.

AI-Humanist Syngenetic Education: An Example of Deep AI-Human Collaboration (corresponding to Discourse 5)

AI-humanist syngenetic education is a model that deeply integrates technology with humanistic values. Its mission is to enhance educational quality while simultaneously preserving human emotion, cultural values, and independent thinking. In the educational system, deep collaboration between AI and humans can be divided into the following areas:

(1) School Administration and Operations

- **AI-Involved Administrative Decision-Making:**

  Student Management: AI data analysis is used to evaluate teaching effectiveness, allocate resources, and assess student needs, thus making the decisions of human administration more scientific.

  Teacher Management: AI analyzes factors such as teachers' abilities, academic backgrounds, personalities, and experiences, and then offers suggestions for class assignments, tutoring groups, internal or external activities, and administrative duties. School leaders then adjust these AI-generated suggestions based on their in-depth observations of each teacher's growth trajectory, before feeding the plan back to AI for further analysis and performance prediction.

- **Smart Campus:**

  Integration of smart devices—such as AI learning platforms and intelligent monitoring systems—to enhance the operational efficiency of the school.

- **Parent-Teacher Communication:**

  AI can establish effective communication channels, analyze students' learning conditions, and help parents and teachers formulate appropriate guidance strategies.

(2) Curriculum Design and Implementation

In the entire curriculum process, it is crucial to have AI participate deeply while retaining humanistic value judgments. The key is clear role division and multi-level involvement.

Curriculum Design:

- **Generative AI for Initial Drafts:**

  Use Generative AI to quickly produce preliminary curriculum outlines, learning objectives, core questions, and activity flows; combine with Open Educational Resources (OER) and other resources (i.e., textbooks and library collections) to automatically compile a repository of multilingual and multicultural learning materials for teacher selection and adaptation.

- **Preview and Integration:**

  Utilize AI to "preview" the curriculum by converting outlines and lesson plans into interactive web templates or integrating them into AI teaching platforms. This allows teachers to verify that the content aligns with subject knowledge, skill development, humanistic ideals, and the objectives of student critical thinking training.

- **Adaptive Learning:**

  Combine with adaptive learning platforms to analyze students' entering standards and needs. AI then automatically suggests teaching progress, class or group arrangements, and adjustments in teaching strategies, ensuring that both common and differentiated learning paths are considered. Teachers modify these suggestions based on their understanding of each student's personality and abilities.

Curriculum Delivery:

- **AI Support in Class:**
  After delivery of learning materials through text, video, audio or activities suggestions, AI chatbots or voice assist students 's learning by providing 24×7 real-time responses to student inquiries and providing supplemental materials. Teachers then focus on deep dialogue and value-based discussions.

- **Automated Translation and Subtitles:**
  Use AI-powered translation and subtitling to present authentic texts or videos in multiple languages (e.g., Chinese, English, and the original language), enabling students to engage directly with primary sources and cross-cultural differences.

- **Interactive Simulations:**
  Employ AI-driven interactive simulations (for example, role-playing or AR/VR-integrated experiences) to simulate historical scenarios or literary worlds, allowing students to immerse themselves in humanistic phenomena. Teachers facilitate on-site reflective and critical discussions.

- **Adaptive Learning Management Systems:**
  Use these systems to tailor instruction based on different abilities and needs. Following AI diagnosis, different learning materials and activities are assigned accordingly.

Assessment of Students and Curriculum:

- **Grading and Analytics:**
  AI automatically produces grading suggestions and statistical charts to help teachers quickly understand students' performance trajectories and common challenges.

- **Automated Assessment of Multimodal Work:**
  AI assesses various student outputs—such as analytical reports, reflective journals, and multimedia creations—providing initial feedback on semantics, structure, and creativity. Teachers then add humanistic value judgments and individualized guidance.

- **Dynamic Learning Portfolios:**
  AI establish portfolios that track the evolution of student work from drafts to revisions to final outputs; AI automatically extracts key growth indicators that serve as material for teacher-student review.

- **AI-Human teacher improvement loop**
  AI collects data and feedback, providing recommendations on improvement of the curriculum. Teachers input human feedback into AI for refinement, fine-tuning and better response.

(3) Student Growth Counseling:

- **Psychological and Emotional Support:**
  AI can analyze fluctuations in student emotions and help teachers and parents provide appropriate psychological counseling and adaptive learning strategies.

- **Promotion of Autonomous Learning:**
  Intelligent learning platforms enable AI to offer feedback and advice, empowering students to manage their own learning more effectively.

- **Development of Social Skills:**
  Although AI can provide language support and cultural guidance, students must cultivate interpersonal communication skills and empathy through direct human interaction.

Teachers should select learning content suggested by AI from a humanistic perspective based on the following principles:

- **Cultural and Ethical Appropriateness:**
  Ensure that AI-proposed learning materials encompass diverse viewpoints and avoid stereotypical biases, and that they do not contravene core values such as human rights or environmental ethics.

- **Depth of Critical Thinking:**
  AI-generated questions or tasks should be seen only as starting points. Teachers must scrutinize for logical gaps or limitations

imposed by current times, and further expand on any implicit assumptions for deeper student evaluation.

- **Contextual Localization:**
  Integrate AI materials with local examples to ensure that learning is relevant to students' lived experiences, thus reinforcing local humanistic care.

- **Narrative Warmth:**
  Compare the tone of AI-generated content with the teacher's instructional style. Teachers should avoid cold, mechanical language by rewriting or adjusting content with their personal "narrative warmth" to maintain the emotional appeal of humanistic subjects.

- **Assessment Alignment:**
  Ensure all AI-assisted evaluation metrics tie in with the institution's "humanistic literacy indicators." Where necessary, teachers should reject or rebuild such standards to prevent purely data-driven evaluations from losing focus.

Through this dual-track "AI + Humanities" co-construction, where AI functions as an "efficiency engine" and "diverse resource pool" and human teachers ensure "value construction" and "critical depth," the core spirit of humanistic education is not only preserved but further amplified and innovated during curriculum design, delivery, and assessment in the AI era.

In this model, school leaders, teachers, parents, and AI collaboratively engage in school management, curriculum design, student growth counseling, and other areas, forming a synergistic effect between artificial intelligence and humanistic education.

Establishing Communication Principles: Enhancing Collaborative Efficiency

To ensure effective collaboration between AI and educational practitioners, certain guiding principles for human-AI collaboration need to be established:

Principle (1) Data-Driven Decision-Making:
All educational improvements must be based on scientific data and empirical research, ensuring that decisions align with educational goals.

Principle (2) – Transparency in AI Operations:
Ensure that teachers, parents, and students can understand how AI functions, and establish trust and oversight mechanisms to prevent the misuse of educational data.

Principle (3) – Real-Time Feedback Mechanisms:
Through AI-powered analysis, teachers can promptly adjust their teaching strategies, and parents can monitor their children's academic progress, ensuring that the educational process meets students' needs.

Principle (4) – Balancing Technology and the Humanities to Build Trust and Emotional Connection:

- **Preserve Humanistic Literacy:**
  AI should assist rather than replace human thought and creativity, ensuring that students continue to develop independent thinking, creativity, and a sense of humanistic care.

- **Address Emotional Needs:**
  While AI provides data analysis, the warmth of interpersonal relationships and emotional communication must be guided by teachers and parents to maintain students' mental health and social skills.

- **Human Value Orientation:**
  All educational decisions should not be based solely on algorithms but must be adjusted and selected in conjunction with human ethics, cultural, and societal values.

The Future of Education is a Symbiosis of Technology and Humanity

"AI-human synergistic education" is not just a technology-driven learning model; it represents an educational revolution that fuses artificial intelligence with human values. In areas such as school administration, curriculum design, and student growth counseling, AI provides efficient and intelligent support. At the same time, teachers and parents are responsible for maintaining the warmth and depth of humanistic education. Through effective communication mechanisms and an empirical foundation based on trusted data, we can establish an educational model that balances technology and the humanities, truly benefiting the growth and development of the next generation.

Conclusion

In the future, the collaboration between AI and humans should resemble a co-creative partnership rather than a simple tool-user dynamic. When AI is capable of offering profound insights, humans must take responsibility for moral considerations, long-term impacts, and emotional judgment to ensure balanced development between technology and society.

Humanity must begin to contemplate such a cooperative model early and establish the necessary educational, legal, and oversight mechanisms. This will ensure that as we enjoy the conveniences and intelligence brought by AI, we also maintain our core human values and autonomy.

Furthermore, once AI handles the training of basic knowledge and skills, the roles of teachers and parents become even more important. They should devote more time and energy to shaping children's character through human-to-human interactions, cultivating empathy and ethical values, guiding cultural transmission, and helping students understand history, philosophy, and values so that the depth of human civilization is maintained. More importantly, through life influencing life, the personal styles of teachers and the behavioral models of parents are irreplaceable factors in a child's developmental process. In the future, rather than simply rushing to achieve academic milestones, teachers and parents will truly concentrate on teaching children how to be good human beings.

Every Child Is Unique

How AI Can Precisely Address Individual Differences and Diverse Learning Needs?

1. **Personalized Learning Analysis and Diagnosis**
   Using big data analytics and machine learning, AI can continuously track each student's learning status. Through online data, assignment performance, test scores, and interactive feedback, AI builds a unique learning profile for each student, identifying their strengths and weaknesses. This not only helps teachers and parents understand a child's learning progress but also enables AI to perform precise, individualized diagnostics during instruction.

2. **Adaptive Learning Environments and Content Adjustment**
   Based on a student's learning state and feedback, the AI system can dynamically adjust course difficulty and the pace of instruction. For example, when a student struggles with a particular chapter, AI can immediately recommend supplementary instructional videos, practice problems, or interactive modules; conversely, for faster learners, it can offer more challenging content. This adaptive learning model allows every child to progress under the right level of challenge—preventing excessive stress while avoiding boredom from overly simple material.

3. **Personalized Learning Path Design**
   Every child has unique interests and potential. AI can plan a bespoke learning path based on a child's interests, talents, and future career tendencies. For instance, in the school case, the older son was directed toward future medical development, while the younger son was steered toward aerospace engineering. Such learning paths are not fixed; they adjust according to a student's performance and evolving interests, ensuring every child can realize their maximum potential at their own pace.

117

4. **Real-Time Feedback and a Bridge for Home–School Communication**

   The AI system can provide immediate feedback, helping students promptly understand their progress and areas for improvement. Simultaneously, through data reports and intelligent alert systems, teachers and parents can obtain detailed insights into a child's learning status, enabling appropriate adjustments and interventions in the home–school collaboration to ensure timely support when difficulties arise.

5. **Emotional Interaction and Motivation Mechanisms**

   Future AI systems will not only focus on knowledge delivery but will also use technologies such as voice and facial expression recognition to sense students' emotional states. When a child feels frustrated or bored, the system can offer encouragement and positive reinforcement, or even recommend engaging learning activities to reignite their passion for learning. This emotional interaction transforms learning from mere data and analysis into an experience filled with warmth and humanized care.

Teachers and parents, faced with the above changes, how will you respond? Feel free to share your thoughts in the space provided below or email me at: aikidsquestion@gmail.com

References

Copilot response, "What might school administration and curriculum look like in 2045 with the integration of AI?" Microsoft, May 16, 2025.

http://www.ibm.com/think/insights/artificial-intelligence-future

http://www.mckinsey.com/capabilities/operations/our-insights/the-future-of-customer-experience-embracing-agentic-ai

Fragiadakis, G., Diou, C., Kousiouris, G., & Nikolaidou, M. (2024). *Evaluating Human-AI Collaboration: A Review and Methodological Framework*. arXiv:2407.19098.

Song, B., Zhu, Q., & Luo, J. (2024). *Human-AI Collaboration by Design*. Cambridge University Press & Assessment.

Spiess, J. (2025, May 27). *Researchers Develop AI Approach with Human Decision-Makers in Mind*. Stanford Graduate School of Business.

Atchley, P., Pannell, H., Wofford, K., Hopkins, M., & Atchley, R. (2024). *Human and AI Collaboration in the Higher Education Environment: Opportunities and Concerns*. Cognitive

Seeber, D. et al. (2020). *Understanding Human-AI Collaboration: A Systematic Review of Challenges and Research Methods in Management*

Chapter 7:
Predicted Scenario (1) of AI–Humanities Synergistic Education: AI-supported Exploration and Nature-Based Learning

Integrating tech and the humanities for a balanced education

Annie is sharing her field study about Yellowstone National Park

"Summer Assignment in 2029"

In the summer of 2029, three classmates—Sammy, Belle and Annie—were given a special learning assignment. They were to collaborate with their friends, families, and AI to select a location in the US or overseas for an experiential field study, then report their findings in September when school resumed. Here are their presentations:

Sammy Report: Giant Panda Conservation Base, Sichuan

"Hi everyone, I am Sammy. I visited the Giant Panda Conservation Base in Sichuan, China, with my family to learn about pandas' living environments. As soon as we arrived, AI helped us identify nearby wildlife and analyze panda behavior. With AI-powered environmental monitoring, I learned how bamboo forest climates affect panda eating habits. Through augmented reality (AR), I even experienced the survival challenges wild pandas face.

What amazed me most was how AI tracked the movement of wild pandas and turned big data into visual charts showing their daily range. This experience deepened my understanding of panda ecology and taught me how to monitor the environment using AI—so cool!

Besides planning our trip and budget with AI, I really appreciated how my teacher later showed me how to analyze environmental data and think about how human behavior affects ecosystems. I also thank my parents for joining me on this journey, encouraging me all the way. We had wonderful conversations and created joyful memories together."

Belly Report: Cultural Impact Study in Hua Hin, Thailand

"Hi, I am Belle. I visited Hua Hin, Thailand, with my family to study how international tourism affects rural culture. With AI's help, I tracked visitor flow data at different times and analyzed popular spots. I also studied how traditional markets changed due to tourist demand.

AI even helped me talk to local residents through real-time translation so I could understand their views on the tourism impact. Some saw tourism as an opportunity for economic growth; others worried it threatened traditional culture. It really got me thinking.

Back home, I used AI to organize my research and built an interactive report. I realized technology is not just a tool. It can help us visualize cultural transformation. My teacher guided me to reflect on the balance between development and cultural preservation. My parents helped me interview locals and encouraged me to understand diverse perspectives. We also tasted many Thai dishes—such a fun and insightful vacation."

Annie's Report: Landscape and ecology in Yellowstone National Park

"Hello everyone, I am Annie! My friends and I visited Yellowstone National Park to study its ecology and geographical features. We used AI to monitor wind-caused weathering and water erosion. We also analyzed the water flow impact on animal life. With drones, we captured changes in mountain and valley topography, and by chatting with an experienced tourist guide. We learned how life has changed over the years.

AI also helped us create a digital photo album—using photos and simulations, we could revisit the history of Yellowstone Park through different eras. I learned not just tech skills, but also how to respect and preserve nature.

In the end, we used AI to simulate possible future developments for the park and explored ways to balance environmental protection with the local economy. I realized tech is not just for innovation—it can help record, analyze, and pass on culture. Thanks to my teacher, who also shared personal stories about visiting the Yellowstone National Park. My friends and I had a blast talking during the trip, and snapping photos—so memorable!"

....

Implementing Human-AI Synergistic Education on Exploration & Nature-based Learning

These three fieldtrips demonstrate how human-AI collaboration can transform education. Future learning is not just tech-driven—it is a partnership between teachers, families, and AI, empowering every student to explore, understand humanity, and nurture wisdom.

When AI takes an active role, learning extends beyond screens into the real world. Students learn through exploration and practice, making knowledge more immersive and personally meaningful. This approach strengthens out-of-classroom education through:

- **AI-Supported Nature Exploration**: Using AR and VR, students get real-time insights into plants, animals, and ecosystems during outdoor excursions.

- **Personalized Learning Journeys**: AI crafts routes and activities tailored to students' interests, turning travel into an engaging educational experience.

- **Cross-Cultural Communication**: AI enables language translation and cultural insights, helping students connect with people from different backgrounds.

- **Learning Feedback & Assessment**: Students generate reports and receive feedback with AI's help, making learning more structured and insightful.

- **Remote Collaboration & Sharing**: AI-powered platforms allow students worldwide to share experiences and co-learn.

AI does not just reshape how we learn—it makes education more interactive, flexible, and global. With AI as a learning partner, students gain richer insights and deeper experiences, truly fulfilling the vision of "learning without boundaries."

The Importance of Authentic Nature Experiences Amidst the Deep Integration of AI in Education

AI-enhanced natural exploration and cultural immersion exemplify "AI–humanities synergistic education," fusing technology with the humanities to make learning deeper, warmer, and more interactive. Beyond its technical role, AI fosters self-directed, personalized learning by tailoring recommendations to each student's interests. For example, an anthropology enthusiast might receive a guided cultural-heritage itinerary. At the same time, an aspiring ecologist could get a custom-designed field-study plan for environmental research, adding both direction and depth to their journey.

Nevertheless, in an era where AI and digital tools play a profound role in education, exposing children to nature and world cultures remains vital to preserving humanity's unique traits. This goes beyond mere knowledge acquisition—it cultivates emotional intelligence, social skills, and creativity.

Balancing Body and Mind: Strengthening Sensory & Emotional Connections

While AI-supported learning excels in efficiency, human senses and emotions still require real-world experiences to develop. Immersion in nature—touching leaves, smelling flowers, listening to bird calls—builds profound emotional bonds with the world, something no algorithm can fully replicate. Such outdoor exploration also relieves digital-fatigue stress, nurturing mental calm and well-being.

Cultivating Social Skills & Empathy Through Genuine Interaction

Technology can bridge distances, but real social skills arise from face-to-face encounters. During travel and fieldwork, students converse with locals and collaborate with peers, learning to listen, appreciate cultural differences, and practice empathy in authentic contexts. While AI can translate language and explain customs, the subtleties of tone, body language, and emotional nuance come only from human interaction.

Sparking Creativity & Critical Thinking

Firsthand observation—watching waterfall formation or city evolution—ignites students' curiosity and creative critical thinking. Although AI supplies data analysis, only on-site experience reveals the true essence of complex challenges. A visit to a region besieged by climate change, for instance, fosters a deeper appreciation for environmental stewardship than statistics alone ever could.

Reinforcing Core Values & Moral Judgment

Encountering diverse cultures and natural landscapes teaches students about different value systems, shaping their moral compass and humanistic thinking. Observing life in underprivileged areas, for example, fosters gratitude for resources and inspires ways to help others. AI provides abundant information, but genuine value judgments arise from lived experience and emotional engagement, nurturing responsible global citizens with both wisdom and compassion.

Deepening Self-Understanding with Tech as a Guide

AI enables personalized learning and world exploration, but true self-knowledge emerges from real-life experiences. In nature or foreign cultures, students discover their passions and values in ways no algorithm can predict: a challenging hike reveals a love of adventure; conversations with strangers spark an interest in cultural studies. These authentic revelations chart each learner's future path.

Synergy Born from Deep AI–Human Collaboration

AI and technology enhance efficiency and personalization, yet emotional growth, social skills, moral reasoning, and creativity still depend on world exploration and firsthand engagement. Integrating AI support with real-world experiences preserves human warmth, wisdom, and perception, shaping well-rounded individuals. Tomorrow's education must blend technological mastery with the full brilliance of humanity.

To orchestrate this synergy in outdoor experiential learning, a **"Before–During–After"** framework with clear roles would help:

1. Pre-Trip Planning

- **AI as Smart Detection & Recommendation Engine:**
  - Analyzes satellite imagery, GIS data, species databases, and cultural, economic, and historical landmarks to generate multiple "learning-route and focal-point" proposals.

- **Teacher's Role:**
  - Refine AI's suggestions through a humanities lens—selecting community narratives, local legends, and student interests to ensure scientific rigor and regional relevance.

2. On-Site Experience

- **Teacher or parent as Humanities Guide:**
  - Poses inquiry prompts (e.g., "Why do certain plants thrive on this slope?"), sparking curiosity.

- **Students as Active Explorers:**
  - Use tablets or smartphones with AI assistants (AR plant and animal ID, acoustic sensors) to gather real-time data. AI returns species info, habits, conservation significance, and suggests "next-step missions" (e.g., locating similar species, recording microclimates).

- **AI Dashboard:**
  - Monitors group progress, enabling teachers to intervene or reallocate resources as needed.

3. Post-Trip Reflection & Assessment

- **Automated AI Reports:**
  - Students upload photos, audio, and notes; AI generates "study-route maps" and "key-findings summaries" with visual links among observations.

- **Teacher-Led Dialogue:**
  - Conduct Socratic discussions on human–environment ethics, local conservation challenges, and action planning.

- **Learning Analytics:**
  - AI tracks indicators (observation acuity, question formulation, teamwork) while teachers add qualitative, humanistic feedback to e-portfolios.

This three-way partnership—AI powering data analysis and personalized guidance, teachers steering values and deep interpretation, students driving exploration and reflection—respects the core of humanities education while maximizing AI's field-application benefits.

Field Learning also Benefits AI

Bringing AI assistants outdoors creates a "human-machine co-learning and continuous optimization" loop:

1. Multimodal Field Data Collection

- Rich inputs (images of flora/insects/terrain, bird calls, GPS tracks, environmental sensors) uploaded by students become fresh AI training samples.

- Students tag AI outputs as correct or incorrect in real time, flagging challenging scenarios (backlighting, overlapping subjects) to build an "error-case library."

2. Human & Student Annotation & Calibration

- Teachers review and enrich annotations with cultural insights and conservation value, embedding humanistic context into the AI's dataset.

3. Incremental Fine-Tuning

- Periodic retraining via incremental or federated learning boosts accuracy for specific regions and seasons without full model overhauls.

- Adversarial training on the "error-case library" hardens the model against tough conditions.

4. Contextualized, Humanized Responses

- AI adapts replies based on location, time, weather, adding local names, indigenous lore, and conservation tips. Each student correction helps the AI co-author a more nuanced, human-centered response style.

5. Performance Monitoring & Iteration

- A dashboard tracks AI accuracy, engagement rates, and student satisfaction across classes and sites. User feedback becomes prioritized feature requests, guiding the development team's roadmap.

Through this five-step cycle—field collection → human annotation → incremental retraining → contextual optimization → performance iteration—AI evolves from a passive tutor to an ever-improving educational partner, delivering:

- More precise, timely species identification
- Responses rich in local culture and ecological values
- Rapid adaptability to new environments

Conclusion

With AI as a supportive guide, humanity can more effectively explore the world's wonders while preserving a focus on culture, emotion, and values, thereby transforming education into a journey that is both intellectually stimulating and emotionally fulfilling. This model nurtures tech-savvy talents who are also empathetic, socially responsible global citizens. AI's role goes beyond mere technical support—it partners with the humanities to make learning an immersive exploration of the world, human nature, and wisdom. When AI, teachers, parents, and students collaborate holistically, education becomes more efficient, healthy, and authentic. Children grow through real-world experiences enriched by technology, developing critical thinking, creativity, and social responsibility—truly realizing an AI-humanities coexistent educational paradigm.

Every Child Is Unique

When rolling out AI-humanities synergistic education and holistic learning strategies, it is essential to honor each student's individual differences and special educational needs, ensuring everyone receives appropriate support. Below are key strategies for addressing diverse learner needs, making education more inclusive, flexible, and personalized:

AI-Powered Personalized Learning

- **Differentiated Instruction**: AI can tailor curricula to a student's learning style, ability, and interests, ensuring each learner studies in the way that suits them best.

- **Adaptive Assessment**: By analyzing progress and comprehension in real time, AI adjusts materials and teaching strategies on the fly, avoiding a one-size-fits-all approach.

Balancing Human Care with Individualized Support

- **Mental Health Support**: AI tools can monitor students' emotional well-being and alert teachers and parents when counseling or emotional support is needed.

- **Maintaining Social Interaction Skills**: While AI aids learning, genuine relationships still form through face-to-face interaction. Teachers should encourage group activities to build social competence.

Diverse Learning Environments & Flexible Models

- **Learning Beyond the Classroom**: Through experiential learning—field trips, outdoor exploration, global cultural exchanges—students develop strengths in varied contexts.

- **Flexible Delivery Modes**: Offer blended online and offline options to accommodate different needs, ensuring adaptability and inclusivity.

Teachers and parents: as you face these educational shifts, how would you respond? Please share your thoughts in the blank space below or email me to discuss:

aikidsquestion@gmail.com

129

References

Copilot response, "How authentic nature learning works with the deep Integration of AI?" Microsoft, May 18, 2025.

http://stemeducationjournal.springeropen.com/articles/10.1186/s405 94-023-00454-3

http://link.springer.com/article/10.1007/s10639-025-13463-2

Chapter 8:
Predicted Scenario (2) of AI–Humanities Synergistic Education: Children and AI Collaborating on STEM Making Activity

Deepen AI Involvement in Human Technological Innovation

"The Three Children's Innovative Aircraft"

John, Ronold, and Henry entered a STEM competition themed "How to Fly with Minimal Pollution." Passionate about aviation technology and environmental protection, they set out to create a genuinely groundbreaking flying device.

At first, John queried the AI for background information and amassed a wealth of existing technical data. Henry then asked the AI to propose a low-pollution aircraft design, but the AI could only regurgitate past products—it did not generate an original concept. Realizing they needed human insight, they consulted their science teacher, Mr.

Smith, who reminded them that the competition's winning entry had to be truly innovative and feasible; mere copying would not suffice.

Ronold had a flash of inspiration: they should visit a real airport to observe current sources of pollution firsthand. There, they carefully noted aircraft noise levels, emissions, and the vast land footprint required for conventional runways. Back at school, they brought their observations to a joint brainstorming session with the AI and Mr. Smith. The AI advised them on refining their craft's aerodynamics to cut drag and energy loss, while Mr. Smith challenged them to envision how future transportation habits might reshape aircraft requirements.

After rounds of spirited debate, sketches, and mutual challenges, the trio finalized a design blueprint for a novel aircraft. They solicited feedback from the AI and Mr. Smith again, iterating until they had built a working scale model. Their design featured:

1. *Streamlined Bio-Inspired Airframe: Mimicking bird wing geometry to minimize drag and maximize energy efficiency.*

2. *Hybrid Low-Emission Propulsion: A mixed electric–hydrogen fuel system paired with regenerative energy recovery to slash carbon output.*

3. *Vertical Take-Off & Landing (VTOL) Capability: Adjustable rotors enabling lift from and touchdown in compact spaces, reducing land use.*

4. *Noise-Reduction Technology: Low-frequency sound-wave suppression mechanisms that greatly cut operational noise, making urban deployment feasible.*

Their innovative model earned second place. Though they did not claim first, they felt immense pride: by combining AI's computational power with human observation and creativity, they had delivered a concept with real future value.

....

This story shows how AI can assist in learning and innovation—yet true breakthroughs stem from human curiosity, reflection, and inventiveness.

AI is a Smart Collaborator

This narrative outlines a new learning paradigm: AI steps beyond a cold tool to become a "smart collaborator," co-driving creative problem-solving alongside teachers and students. Here's how the three children's innovation journey unfolded:

1. Real-World Context
   Upon learning the contest theme, students first gathered data via AI. Thinking AI alone could deliver the final design, they soon realized, through Mr. Smith's guidance, that firsthand observation was essential. Visiting the airport nurtured their curiosity and independent thinking, embodying the spirit of inquiry-based education.

2. Humanistic Guidance
   From a humanities perspective, Mr. Smith urged them to reflect on how future travel habits influence design—and, crucially, to prioritize originality over imitation. Through teacher-student debates and challenges, they cultivated reflective thinking and the interpersonal skills central to human culture.

3. AI-Driven Technical Input & Decision Support
   The AI rapidly aggregated and organized specialized knowledge, streamlining airframe concepts, noise-reduction methods, and more by filtering massive datasets, allowing the team to focus on core questions. When the students proposed initial solutions, the AI evaluated their feasibility and resource demands.

4. Collaborative Design Cycle
   Students sketched and built models, then used AI simulations for aerodynamics and energy-consumption analysis. With multi-angled feedback from both AI and Mr. Li, they continuously refined their design until it achieved genuine innovation.

This STEM project became a testament to deep human–AI collaboration. AI not only executed technical tasks but also tailored solutions to meet the team's evolving needs and participated in decision-making. Humans, in turn, defined the project's values and meaning, ensuring technology served real human aspirations.

Such "AI–humanities synergistic education" does not merely teach children how to build—it guides them to understand why they build, emphasizing the ethical, social, and humanistic dimensions underpinning technology.

Design Thinking Meets AI–Humanities Synergistic Education

If we weave MIT's Design Thinking framework into AI-driven STEM education. In that case, we underscore the power of deep AI-human collaboration, which boosts students' innovation skills while reinforcing humanistic values and attentiveness to real human needs.

Below is a story that illustrates how the five stages of Design Thinking, together with intensive AI involvement, bring AI-Humanities Synergistic Education to life:

"All-Weather Wheelchair for the Elderly"

Today, Ms. Davis announced the semester's tech project: design an all-weather wheelchair for seniors with limited mobility—one that keeps out rain, resists wind and slips, and remains both safe and comfortable. Even more, students must follow MIT's five Design Thinking steps in partnership with an AI assistant. High-schooler Rex and his younger sister Yan were thrilled by the challenge but nervous—they loved tech but knew nothing about mobility aids for the elderly.

1. Empathize

Ms. Davis led the class to interview Mr. White, a neighbor who suffers from partial paralysis after a stroke. Armed with tablets, Rex and Yan used their AI helper "X partner" to transcribe her words, detect her tone and facial expressions, and tag emotions in real time. X partner distilled Mr. White's challenge—fear of slipping in the rain and discomfort from a too-hard seat cushion—and mapped out her psychological needs: *"I need to feel safe going out in the rain"* and *"I need a backrest that flexes just enough."*

2. Define

Building on X partner's interview summary, Ms. Davis guided students to frame the core challenge as a *"How might we…"* question:

How might we design an all-weather wheelchair that stays dry and slip-resistant in wet conditions, yet remains comfortable even after long periods of sitting?

X partner then surfaced historical case studies and relevant patents, and used NLP to condense 50+ research papers into a two-page slide deck—giving students a sharp problem definition.

3. Ideate

On the whiteboard, Rex sketched keywords like *"waterproof canopy,"* *"retractable footplate,"* and *"active shock sensors."* Yan fed these ideas to X partner, asking it to generate 50 different concept sketches via an image-generation model. The AI also suggested bio-inspired details—lotus-root–style drainage holes and carbon-fiber anti-slip treads. Together, the students and AI filtered through hundreds of sketches to identify the three most promising concepts.

4. Prototype

In the school's AI-powered fabrication lab, they imported the winning concepts into an AI-driven CAD system for structural optimization, topology analysis, and load simulations. After minor manual tweaks, Rex hit *"Print."* A few hours later, the team had a physical prototype: a waterproof canopy, a bendable backrest, and a chassis with built-in sensor ports for later testing.

5. Test

They wheeled the prototype to Mr. White's home. X partner recorded data on wet-surface grip, canopy leak points, and vibration levels across slopes. Mr. White tried it herself, scoring her comfort and confidence via mood icons on a tablet. The AI merged objective measurements with her subjective feedback into an *"Improvement Report."*

It found excellent traction but noted water pooling at seam joints; the seat was soft enough overall but lacked edge support.

Back to ideation: this time, X partner proposed invisible drainage valves at the seams and 2D-scanned cushion edges for shape optimization. After a second round of 3D printing and testing, Mr. White beamed approval.

Throughout the journey, X partner handled complex data crunching and rapid simulations; Ms. Davis ensured the team never lost sight of human dignity and user values; and Rex and Yan learned not only engineering principles but also the essence of human-centered design. When Mr. White rolled confidently in the drizzle, waving with a smile, the seamless synergy of AI and humanistic education was their warmest reward.

The future all-weather wheelchair

The mission—to design an "all-weather wheelchair" for seniors with limited mobility that keeps out rain, resists wind and slipping, and remains comfortable and safe—combines MIT's five Design Thinking steps with deep AI collaboration. It vividly illustrates the value of AI-Humanities Synergistic Education.

1. Empathize—Human-Centered Understanding

- Field Interviews & Observation

  - Take students into nursing centers and the community to interview elders and caregivers, uncovering real frustrations—getting soaked while waiting, swaying in gusts, wheels slipping.

- Scenario Simulation + AI Assistance

  - Use VR/AR to immerse students in "riding in the rain" and "strong-wind" scenarios so they viscerally feel seniors' fears.

  - Apply AI–driven sentiment analysis to interview transcripts, tagging negative keywords (e.g., "fear," "cold," "unstable") to highlight the most urgent pain points.

AI-humanities-synergy meaning: Students empathize deeply with elders' emotional needs—focusing not only on technical fixes but on user dignity and safety.

2. Define—Focusing on Core Needs

- Problem Statement
  - After data collection and synthesis, craft a clear brief:

  - "How might we design an all-weather wheelchair for seniors over 75 with mobility impairments that remains stable, slip-resistant, waterproof, and cold-proof in wind and rain?"

- AI–Powered Research Filtering

  - AI rapidly scans existing solutions, such as rain-proof canopies, all-terrain tires, and folding shields, annotating pros and cons so students spot market gaps.

AI-humanities synergy meaning: AI processes vast information volumes, but teachers and students jointly define the "value proposition," ensuring solutions truly meet human needs.

3. Ideate—Generating Diverse Concepts

- Brainstorming Workshop

  - In teams, students apply SCAMPER and reverse brainstorming to propose ideas: detachable rain hoods, aerodynamic wind vanes, auto-leveling suspension, multi-directional slip-resistant wheels.

- AI-Assisted Concept Generation

  - AI supplies analogies (lotus-leaf water-repellent surfaces, self-orienting wind turbines) and uses generative models to produce dozens of concept sketches combining materials and structures.

AI-humanities synergy meaning: AI acts as a creative catalyst, while students retain critical judgment and choice, yielding richer, more nuanced designs.

4. Prototype—Quickly Validating Ideas

1. Physical Mock-Ups

   - Students build low-fidelity models from cardboard, PVC, and plastic sheeting, then attach rubber treads for simple slip tests.

2. AI-Driven Simulation

   - On an AI-integrated CFD cloud platform, simulate rain impact and wind loads to analyze drag coefficient (Cd) and stress distribution.

   - AI's machine-learning optimizer refines canopy curves and support angles, producing an "optimized first draft" for students to review.

AI-humanities synergy meaning: AI accelerates iteration; hands-on prototyping deepens students' understanding of the interplay among user, product, and environment.

5. Test—Review & Redesign

1. User Trials

- Invite elders to test the prototype, measuring seating stability, water ingress, and push-effort; record their real-time feedback via an AI voice assistant.

2. AI Data Analysis

- AI consolidates results into comfort "heatmaps," waterproofing curves, and thrust-requirement charts, helping students see strengths and weaknesses objectively.

3. Humanistic Reflection

- Teachers guide a discussion on dignified senior mobility—considering future smart-community transport and barrier-free infrastructure—and feed these insights into the next iteration.

AI-humanities synergy meaning: AI's data drives improvements, while teachers and students ensure each tweak is grounded in elders' well-being and dignity.

Generating AI-Human Synergy

MIT's Design Thinking is already an effective human-centered STEM creation approach. Adding a deep AI partnership transforms it into a powerful model of AI–humanities synergistic education. In the "All-Weather Wheelchair" project, synergy emerges through:

1. Role Definition & Complementary Strengths

- AI integrates data (sentiment tags, literature summaries), generates sketches, runs simulations, and streams sensor feedback.

- Teacher (Ms. Davis): frames human-centered interviews, safeguards values/ethics, leads Socratic challenges to AI outputs, and infuses local and cultural context.

- Students conduct interviews, feed ideas to AI, co-ideate, build prototypes, and gather user feedback.

2. Continuous Iteration & Closed-Loop Feedback

- Real-time AI transcription and tagging → human correction & annotation → AI optimization creates a rapid "collect → annotate → refine" cycle.

- Post-test AI reports fuse quantitative metrics with user satisfaction, guiding each redesign to align closely with elders' needs.

3. Parallel Humanities & Technical Precision

- AI's cold-hard data and sketches gain narrative warmth through teacher-student storytelling—preserving the humanities core.

- Each human-guided tweak enriches AI's locale-specific dataset, boosting recognition accuracy and simulation fidelity.

4. Dual Benefits: Project Learning & AI Self-Improvement

- Students master the full design-thinking cycle that includes empathy, ideation, prototyping, and iteration while internalizing humanistic values.

- AI learns from teacher and student annotations, feedback, and real-world corrections, becoming ever more robust and user-sensitive.

In this way, AI transcends mere "tool" status to become a true collaborator—co-collecting, analyzing, designing, testing, and iterating with teachers and students. This three-way collaboration yields an all-weather wheelchair that marries technical precision with human warmth, vividly demonstrating the transformative power of AI–humanities synergistic education.

Conclusion

AI is reshaping every industry—from medical diagnostics to autonomous driving, machines can replace rote physical labor and also assist in complex analysis. Traditional "rote memorization plus single-subject" education can no longer keep pace with rapid change. Students must develop "human–machine collaboration" skills: mastering AI tools while applying a humanistic, critical framework to judge technology's impact. That is precisely why we emphasize STEM and innovation education.

"AI–humanities synergistic education" honors both people and technology: it prevents children from becoming mere machine operators and ensures inventions retain a human touch. Guided jointly by AI assistants and human teachers, students learn to innovate boldly and reflect deeply on technology's social and environmental responsibilities. Through iterative project experiences, they come to value "the lessons of failure" and welcome "diverse feedback," equipping them to adapt swiftly to new tools and methods in tomorrow's workforce. The truly irreplaceable talent of the future will not be those displaced by AI, but those who walk alongside AI, using it to amplify human compassion and creative power.

"AI–humanities synergistic education" goes beyond teaching STEM. It teaches students to become fully human, tech-empowered citizens. That is the most precious gift we can offer the AI generation.

Every Child Is Unique

Implementing AI–humanities synergistic education and holistic learning strategies demands attention to each student's individual differences and special educational needs. The following five mechanisms ensure inclusivity, flexibility, and personalization:

1. **Learner Profile**

- Use an AI platform to gather each student's background (interests, strengths, weaknesses, learning history) along with pre-tests and surveys to build a dynamic knowledge map.
- Update continuously: every quiz, discussion, or prototype yields data points that AI captures to refine each learner's profile.

2. **Adaptive Learning Path**

- Layered content delivery: based on ability, AI recommends content at foundational, intermediate, or challenge levels—videos, simulations, and exercise sets tailored to each student.
- Real-time remediation or extension: if a student struggles with any technology module, AI prompts a targeted review; if they finish early, AI suggests advanced projects or open-ended explorations.

3. **Multiple Presentations and Flexible assignment**

- Multiple representations: AI presents the same STEM concept via animation, 3D models, text, and micro-lectures so learners of different learning styles all thrive.
- Flexible assignments: students choose from writing a report, recording a tutorial video, or building a prototype and filming it; AI aligns rubrics with the chosen format and compiles feedback for the teacher's human-centered evaluation.

4. **Collaborative Projects & Peer/AI Tutoring**

- AI-driven group formation: matching students with complementary skills and interests to ensure mutual support in every team.
- AI teaching assistant and peer coach roles: an AI chatbot offers 24/7 conceptual help, while outstanding peers may become certified "AI Peer Tutors," mentoring classmates and earning micro-credits.

5. Formative Assessment & Reflection

- Real-time analytics: an AI dashboard tracks participation, concept mastery, and learning curves, empowering teachers to fine-tune pacing and strategy.

- Reflection prompts: AI regularly reminds students to journal—What did I learn today? Where am I stuck? How will I improve? — fostering self-monitoring and metacognitive growth.

Through these five pillars, AI–Humanities Synergistic Education not only personalizes STEM content but also preserves the deep human bond between teachers and individual students. AI serves as "data chef" and "on-demand tutor," while teachers focus on value-centered guidance and empathetic support; together crafting each child's most effective learning blueprint.

Teachers and parents, as you face the transformations described above, how will you respond? Share your thoughts in the blank space below, or email me at:
aikidsquestion@gmail.com

References

Copilot response, "How to deepen AI involvement in human technological Innovation?" Microsoft, May 19, 2025.

https://news.mit.edu/2025/mit-students-works-redefine-human-ai collaboration-0129

https://education.mit.edu/project/collaborative-ai-for-learning-cail/

https://design.mit.edu/news/mit-students-work-redefine-human-ai-collaboration-at-neurips

https://cognitiveresearchjournal.springeropen.com/articles/10.1186/s 41235-024-00547-9

https://link.springer.com/content/pdf/10.1007/s40593-023-00356-z.pdf

https://acceleratelearning.stanford.edu/story/the-future-is-already-here-ai-and-education-in-2025/

Chapter 9:
Predicted Scenario (3) of
AI–Humanities Synergistic Education:
Service Learning That Never Fades

Learning through making meaningful contributions

Kate is leading the way for the two girls.

Olivia lives in England; she had always found history class dull—just rote memorization. But one unexpected experience changed her mind completely.

One day, their history teacher, Mr. Peterson, assigned each student a month-long research project on a topic of their choice. He suggested they first consult AI to help pick and plan their study. Olivia thought, "Why not?" She fed the assignment details and Mr. Peterson's criteria into the AI. Within moments, the AI generated a full

145

report on "The Black Country in England"—then added, "This report meets your requirements. Have you considered doing a hands-on field study yourself?" That last line surprised Emma.

On Saturday, she and her close friend Emma set out to hike in a mountain near Birmingham. By midday, they had wandered into dense woods and realized they were lost. Luckily, they met an eighty-year-old lady, Kate, who guided them two hours back to the main trail. Along the way, Kaite wove stories of Birmingham's past—the bustling old market, hidden wartime passages, and how coal miners banded together in hard times. Olivia was spellbound; these living memories were far richer than any textbook.

Two days later, inspired, Olivia and Emma told Mr. Peterson they wanted to research "Old Birmingham" by interviewing Kate. Mr. Peterson approved—and challenged them to focus on one additional goal: how could their historical study benefit Kate? They wondered: How does history benefit an elderly woman?

Guided by Mr. Peterson and AI, they drafted interview questions. The AI not only supplied key queries and multimedia on Birmingham's history but coached them on deep-listening techniques—how to ask follow-up questions that draw out emotion and how to show respectful empathy.

During the interview, Kate warmly shared memories of Old Birmingham's heyday, the toil of coal mining, and the way miners protected their community even during wars. Her stories carried real emotion and weight. On the final day, she recalled working long hours in the mine alongside her late parents and husband; tears welled, then fell. Grasping Olivia and Emma's hands, she choked out, "It's been so long since anyone truly listened... Thank you both, thank you."

In that moment, Olivia and Emma understood Mr. Peterson's lesson: this was not just history—it was service. By listening, they honored Kate's life story and made her feel valued.

They no longer saw history as cold facts in a book but as living memories rooted in people and place. History, they discovered, has warmth.

Epilogue
After submitting their report, Olivia and Emma launched a community-interview project, inviting classmates to record stories from local elders—turning history into a bridge that connects generations. Mr. Peterson watched with a smile, knowing his lesson in humanities had taken root.

....

What Is Service Learning?

Service learning has a long history as a curricular and pedagogical approach. It is an educational model that integrates "community service" with "learning," enabling students to deepen their knowledge, skills, and values through hands-on service. This "learning by doing" approach not only applies classroom concepts to real-life situations but also cultivates empathy, responsibility, and civic engagement.

How Service Learning Shows Up in the Story

In Olivia and Emma's experience, they initially set out merely to complete a history report. Yet, through interviewing Kate, they realized their project was more than just academic research—it was a service. By giving Kate the chance to tell her story and feel truly heard and respected, they embodied the core value of service-learning: serving others as a path to deeper learning.

Mr. Peterson's guidance also reflected the spirit of humanistic education. He urged them to ask how their research could actually benefit Kate, helping them see that history is not only an accumulation of facts but a bridge for human connection. This approach fosters social responsibility, transforming learning from mere knowledge acquisition into meaningful contribution.

Using AI to enhance values-based community service and learning

Artificial intelligence plays a key role at each phase of service learning—preparing students, supporting them during service, and helping them apply what they have learned in community projects. Its functions include:

1. AI–Assisted Preparation (Learn for Service)

• Data Gathering & Analysis: AI compiles community history, social issues, and policy contexts so students gain key insights quickly.

• Personalized Learning: Based on interests and needs, AI recommends articles, videos, and case studies that target each student's knowledge gaps.

• Simulated Practice: Chatbot interfaces let students rehearse interviews, sharpening their communication skills before meeting service recipients.

2. AI–Supported Service (Learn through Service)

• Interview Design: AI helps craft structured, in-depth questions to guide meaningful conversations.

• Real-Time Translation & Speech Recognition: Enables cross-lingual communication with diverse community members.

• Sentiment Analysis: AI analyzes tone and emotion in responses, helping students more keenly perceive service recipients' needs and feelings.

3. AI–Facilitated Application (Learning by Applying Knowledge)

• Identifying Service Opportunities: AI matches students' skills with community needs, analyzes those needs, and suggests service plans.

• Community Research Projects: Students can use AI-supported monitoring methods—e.g., measuring local air or noise pollution and generating reports for relevant authorities.

- Ongoing Reflection: AI prompts students to reflect on how their service leveraged learned skills and offers personalized suggestions for further growth.

AI–Human Deep Interaction

A pivotal moment in the story comes when the AI, having produced an "Black Country of England" report, asks Olivia, *"Have you considered doing a hands-on field study yourself?"* This kind of follow-up question reflects advanced AI capabilities, including:

1. Conversational AI

- Natural Language Processing and Dialogue Management let the AI understand context and pose timely questions to deepen engagement.

2. Active Learning

- By asking for more input, the AI gathers additional data to refine its own understanding and improve future responses.

3. Human–AI Collaboration

- The AI's questions position it as a partner in exploration, not merely a tool—an approach akin to decision-support systems where human insight and AI analysis co-produce solutions.

4. Social Dialogue Modeling

- Context awareness enables the AI to mimic human social cues, deciding when a reflective question will enrich the conversation.

5. Metacognition

- Adaptive learning systems let the AI assess its own knowledge limits and solicit user feedback when uncertain, driving continual improvement.

Such interactive questioning transforms the exchange into a collaborative, intelligent dialogue rather than a one-way instruction. It exemplifies our discourse (4) insight that we must develop high-level human–AI collaboration modes as AI increasingly joins decision-making. By prompting students to pursue their own fieldwork, this AI demonstrates a humanizing touch. If schools, teachers, and parents embrace similar interactions, children will collaborate more fruitfully with AI—and reap the full benefits.

AI–Supported Service Learning: A Paradigm of AI–Humanities Synergistic Education

Integrating AI into Service Learning is a typical example of "AI–humanities synergistic education." It not only leverages AI to boost learning effectiveness but also cultivates students' social responsibility and humanistic care.

1. AI Fosters Deep Learning and Community Service

AI can help students conduct research and analysis more efficiently, for example:

- Interview Preparation: AI assists in crafting structured, in-depth interview questions.

- Data Organization & Analysis: AI quickly collates respondents' answers, helping students grasp historical and community contexts.

- Community Connection: AI identifies additional groups in need, extending the reach and impact of service learning.

With AI's support, students not only complete tasks more efficiently but also gain a deeper understanding of community needs—transforming service learning from mere academic research into genuine social contribution.

2. AI Strengthens the Humanistic Core of Service Learning

Humanities education emphasizes empathy, social responsibility, and independent thinking. AI applications in service learning advance these values by:

- Cultivating Empathy: AI analyzes community issues so students can better appreciate interviewees' circumstances and emotions.

- Enhancing Social Responsibility: Through AI-driven data analysis, students discern trends in social problems and contemplate how to contribute.

- Promoting Independent Thought: AI provides diverse information sources, compelling students to evaluate credibility and sharpen critical thinking.

In Olivia and Emma's story, they used AI to design interview guides and organize findings—and discovered that service learning was not just about studying history but about caring for Kate. They learned that knowledge is not confined to textbooks but serves as a bridge for human connection. This is the essence of "AI–humanities synergistic education": AI becomes more than a technical tool—it is a medium for humanistic care, making learning both knowledge acquisition and social responsibility in action.

Next-Gen Service Learning in the AI Era

Service Learning in the AI age can adopt new hybrid models across three phases— "Pre-Service Diagnosis," "Collaborative Practice," and "Post-Service Reflection":

1 Data-Driven Needs Assessment

- AI-Powered Data Analysis: AI gathers and analyzes public data (e.g., social-welfare reports, community sentiment) to map the needs of seniors, minorities, and special-needs families.

- Dashboard Insights: Students use an AI dashboard to visualize "most urgent issues" and "service hotspots," enabling precise project scoping.

2 AI-Augmented Hybrid Service

- Virtual Micro-Volunteers: AI chatbots and voice bots offer 24/7 companionship for isolated elders—guiding exercises, conversational practice, and daily wellness check-ins.

- On-Site AI Assistants: During field visits, workshops, or classes, AI acts as a real-time teaching assistant—providing translation and data lookup so students can focus on human interaction and care.

3 Intelligent Micro-Services

- On-Demand Mini-Apps: AI-driven apps push daily care tasks (e.g., community disinfection, senior-center visits), enabling volunteers to take action with a single tap.

- Automated Environmental Monitoring: AI image-recognition scans for community problems (potholes, lack of greenery), with students interpreting findings and organizing improvement efforts.

4 AI-Supported Meta-Learning & Deep Reflection

- Interactive Reflection Journals: AI generates templates to guide students through systematic self-examination of ethical dilemmas, cultural nuances, and human–AI collaboration gaps.

- Personalized Feedback: AI analyzes journal entries—text or voice—to score empathy, assess communication effectiveness, and suggest tailored growth pathways.

5 Co-Creation Platform: AI–Human–Community Dialogue

- Collaborative Online Hub: AI, students, and community elders co-design projects: AI synthesizes discussion points, students coordinate resources and activities, and elders contribute local wisdom and feedback.

- Impact Tracking & Iteration: The platform auto-metrics participation, satisfaction, and community impact—fueling ongoing optimization and truly embodying "service is learning, learning is service."

By embracing these new models, service learning evolves from a one-way "students helping the community" into a dynamic cycle of co-creation among AI, humans, and the community—striking a balance between efficiency and warmth while embedding humanistic care and social responsibility.

Conclusion

Integrating AI into service learning is an outstanding example of "AI–humanities synergistic education," because it not only embeds technology into learning and service but also fosters deep collaboration among teachers, students, and AI. Together, they co-create decisions, generate synergy, and serve the well-being of individuals and society.

AI helps students conduct research and analysis more effectively. With AI's assistance, students not only complete tasks more efficiently but also gain deeper insight into service recipients' needs—transforming service learning from pure academic research into a genuine contribution to humanity.

These innovative service-learning models significantly boost efficiency while making AI a powerful amplifier of humanistic care, strengthening community bonds and shared well-being. Thanks to AI, service learning no longer merely enhances academic outcomes; it guides students to recognize social needs in practice and cultivates empathy and social responsibility. By marrying AI with humanities education, we infuse learning with deeper meaning and help students grow into empathetic, socially responsible citizens.

Since its emergence in the 1950s in America, service learning has become a timeless educational pedagogy. As we enter the AI era, blending this "veteran" of education with cutting-edge AI will forge an enduring, high-quality learning solution.

Every Child Is Unique

When implementing service learning, it is vital to address each student's individual differences. Here are some concrete practices:

1. Preliminary Needs & Competency Assessment

- Use surveys, interviews, or small-group discussions to identify students' interests, strengths, language abilities, and learning needs.

- Based on the diagnosis, collaborate with each student to set "baseline goals" and "challenge goals," allowing them to progress at their own pace.

2. Tiered Instruction & Tiered Tasks

- Design "core tasks" and "value-added tasks" at two levels according to students' abilities, experience, or interests—enabling stronger students to dive deep while others solidify foundations.

- Both tiers center on a shared theme (e.g., documenting community history) but offer flexible choices in tools, research methods, and presentation formats.

3. Diversified Assessment & Dynamic Support

- Employ multiple assessment modes—oral presentations, written reports, multimedia records, so learners of different expression styles can showcase their achievements.

- Combine peer review, teacher–student dialogues, and self-assessment to adjust pacing and support resources adaptively.

4. Group Collaboration & Role Assignment

- Form heterogeneous teams so students with complementary strengths—interviewing, data synthesis, tech/multimedia—support one another.

- Teachers or aides circulate among groups, providing strategic guidance and emotional support to ensure equity and attention to every member.

Teachers and parents, as you confront the transformations outlined above, how will you respond? Please share your thoughts below or email me: aikidsquestion@gmail.com

References:

Copilot response, "How to deepen AI involvement in services learning?" Microsoft, May 21, 2025.

http://www.edb.gov.hk/tc/curriculum-development/4-key-tasks/moral-civic/Newwebsite/flash/servicelearning/service learning.html

https://dpi.wi.gov/service-learning/about#:~:text=Service%2DLearning%20is%20a%20form,to%20address%20genuine%20community%20needs.

https://nces.ed.gov/surveys/frss/publications/1999043/index.asp?sectionid=5

Chapter 10:
A New Model of Home Education with Parent–AI Collaboration

Illusory Learning

Joe thinks, "I've been relying on AI and haven't really learned anything myself."

"AI Does the Work—But Did Your Child Really Learn?!"

At the start of the term, Joe sat at his desk and muttered, "This math problem is so hard… I will just ask AI."
The AI responded instantly and clearly. Joe's eyes lit up: "Wow—it not only solves the problem; it even walks me through every step! Amazing!"

A few weeks later, his mother noticed that Joe always finished his homework in record time.

"Joe, have you already done your assignments today?" she asked.

"Yeah—AI did them for me!" he replied with a grin.

His father frowned. "You mean... You just have AI do your homework?"

Joe bristled. "But I still learn! I look at how it works."

On exam day, the classroom was deathly silent. Joe stared at the math questions, sweat beading his brow.

"I've seen this before... but how do I actually solve it myself?" he panicked.

When it came to the essay writing, he gripped his pen but could not write a word.

"What do I do... I always let AI write my essays. I... I do not even know how to start."

That evening, the family gathered to see the results. The mood was heavy.

His mother studied the report card, voice soft: "Joe, what happened?"

Joe lowered his head, thinking, "I've been leaning on AI—there's nothing I truly learned myself."

His father spoke firmly: "We're not against you using AI, but you can't live your life by it alone."

His mother gently patted his shoulder: "AI is a tool. It will not make you grow, learn from mistakes, or build perseverance. We want you to solve problems on your own first—and then use AI to check your work."

Tears in his eyes, Joe nodded. "I understand. From now on, I will try it myself first, then ask AI to check."

From that day on, a new voice echoed through the house:

"Mom, did I solve this question correctly? I tried it myself, then I asked AI—and it showed me another method! That is pretty cool!"

His mother smiled. "This is the learning we want to see!"

....

This story highlights how overdependence on AI can turn learning into a superficial exercise rather than a deep, lasting process. Joe began by using AI as a helpful assistant—checking steps and gathering information—but his growing reliance ultimately eroded his own capacity to think and solve problems. When faced with unprepared situations, such as exams, his gaps in understanding became apparent, triggering a real learning crisis.

By dramatizing Joe's struggles with math and his paralysis over the writing task, the narrative vividly illustrates how leaning too heavily on AI robs students of the "painful growth" that comes from tackling challenges head-on. His parents' intervention makes clear that this dependency produces only the illusion of progress, denying learners the chance to self-verify and internalize knowledge. In turn, it undermines both deep mastery and critical thinking.

The core message is this: technology should serve as a learning aid, not a shortcut that replaces thought and practice. True growth arises from hands-on exploration, making mistakes, and then correcting them. Parents, acting as gatekeepers and guides, play an indispensable role in their children's journey toward maturity. Even in an era when AI tools proliferate and tempt us with instant solutions, vigilant parents must uphold firm principles and invest time in overseeing their children's education—both in school and beyond—to ensure genuine development in knowledge, skills, and character.

Preventing Superficial Learning

Ethan Mollick, an AI researcher, used the term "illusory learning" to shake us out of the current AI craze. He warns of the serious consequences when students rely heavily on AI without proper guidance. His findings show that, because external tools like AI let students finish assignments and tasks quickly, they appear to master the learning, but in reality, their ability to internalize knowledge, understand concepts deeply, and train critical thinking remains unimproved. This creates the illusion that neat homework and high grades equal genuine learning. Yet when students must apply knowledge independently—in an exam or real-world problem—they often discover they lack the necessary understanding and skills.

Mollick observes that when learners over-depend on AI—using chatbots or other automation to gather information, solve problems, or write essays—they merely go through the motions. This dependency sharply reduces opportunities for active thinking and hands-on practice, giving rise to what he calls "illusory learning." A related phenomenon, the "illusion of explanatory depth," occurs when individuals believe they understand a topic far more deeply than they actually do. The result is predictable: when true independent thought is required, such as solving novel exam questions or composing an original essay, students underperform. In today's digital and AI-enhanced educational environment, illusory learning has become a hidden yet pervasive risk.

To counteract it, Mollick advocates designing instruction that breaks the illusion. For example, teachers might require students to attempt problems on their own first, then use AI to verify and extend their solutions. This approach harnesses technology's strengths without letting learners slip into mere tool dependence that robs them of skill development.

Mollick's insights serve as a powerful warning for modern education: as information technology accelerates, we must strike a balance between tech assistance and students' own drive to learn.

Strategies to prevent illusory learning in school

The more powerful and tempting AI becomes, the more likely children may fall into the trap of superficial learning—thinking they have mastered something when, in reality, they have only gained a misleading sense of competence. Schools must take action to guide children back to authentic learning. Below are strategies schools can adopt to help children avoid this illusion of understanding:

Focus on Process, Not Just Answers

- Encourage children to explain how they arrived at their answers—not just whether it is right or wrong, but how they think.
- Ask them to explain verbally or show their work by writing out calculations.
- This helps reduce over-reliance on AI-generated answers.

Use Open-Ended Questions

- Avoid simple true/false or single-choice questions.
- Pose questions that require reasoning, analysis, or personal reflection to prompt deeper thinking.

Add Extension Tasks

- If children use AI to gather information, ask them to:
- Take notes
- Summarize what they learned
- Rephrase key points in their own words
- Draw diagrams
- Teach you the concept they just learned

Assess True Understanding

- See if your child can "teach" the concept to someone else—explaining it clearly to a peer or adult indicates real comprehension.
- Try "flipped teaching": let the child take on the role of the teacher.
- Include intentional errors or flawed examples and see if your child can identify and correct them.
- Test their ability to apply knowledge across varied scenarios to gauge flexibility in understanding.

Diagnose the Issue & Evaluate Progress

- Observe homework and test performance.
- Compare results when AI assistance is used vs. when it is not, to identify where misconceptions or knowledge gaps appear.

Engage in Reflective Conversations

- Review the questions your child asked the AI, the responses they received, and how they used or adapted that information.
- This helps distinguish passive copying from active learning.

Home as the Final Fortification: The Family's Compensatory Education

In the battle against illusory learning, the family plays a critical "last line of defense," helping children learn authentically rather than simply leaning on tech shortcuts. As AI's allure grows ever more powerful, children's illusory learning becomes increasingly common. Hence, beyond urgent compensatory measures in schools, families must also provide compensatory education. Once we identify which skills or traits children risk losing through AI overuse, families need to fill those gaps. Below, we consolidate earlier learning strategies into effective family-based compensatory education methods.

Here are several strategies parents can use:

1. Foster Open Communication

Maintain honest, ongoing dialogues about how your child uses AI and digital tools. Ask questions like, "How did you think through this problem?" or "Which parts of AI's answer do you really understand?" Such conversations reveal hidden learning gaps and encourage reflection, turning answers into internalized knowledge rather than passive receipt.

2. Encourage Hands-On Activities

Balance screen time with physical, real-world experiences: family book clubs, kitchen-table science experiments, or outdoor explorations. These varied contexts deepen learning, tempering the lure of online AI tools and building a well-rounded skill set.

3. Model Lifelong Learning

When parents themselves demonstrate curiosity—sharing problem-solving experiences, reading insights, and tackling new topics alongside their kids—they ignite enthusiasm for genuine inquiry. Leading by example shows that true growth comes from sustained practice and reflection.

4. Authentic Learning

Authentic learning is an educational approach that immerses students in real-world tasks closely tied to their lives, fostering deep and lasting knowledge and skills. It values the learning process—problem-solving, application, and internalization—over mere outcomes. To counter illusory learning, authentic learning experiences (like field visits into nature, hands-on STEM projects, and service learning) let kids feel the joy and meaning of learning firsthand.

5. Field Visits & Nature Immersion

When children engage with real environments—ancient towns, museums, or natural landscapes—they use multiple senses to observe how things work. These experiences reveal knowledge's sources and complexity, beyond what digital data or instant answers can offer. Observing wildlife or feeling weather changes nurtures curiosity and respect for nature, compensating for AI's shallow "instant-answer" trap. Parents play a vital role here: unlike schools that offer occasional trips, they can regularly take kids on weekend and holiday outings, guiding observations, storytelling, and probing questions.

6. Service Learning

Service learning lets children apply classroom knowledge to real community needs—through volunteering or environmental projects—demonstrating how ideas translate into action and fostering empathy and civic responsibility. Such human interaction starkly contrasts with AI's surface-level answers. Parents planning meaningful service activities—

especially involving family members or local elders—add emotional depth and greater impact.

By orchestrating these authentic learning experiences alongside AI's support, families help children develop independent thinking, problem-solving skills, and interpersonal capabilities—capacities that digital tools alone cannot instill. These deep, immersive experiences yield vibrant, internalized knowledge and offset the illusory learning created by AI dependence.

Family–AI Collaborative Education

Just as schools harness AI for AI–humanities synergistic education, families too can forge high-level partnerships with AI, creating environments that foster genuine, deep learning. Here are strategies for parents:

1. Co-Learn with AI as Facilitator
   Parents should master AI's strengths and limits to guide children effectively. Use AI together—fetching information or solving problems—but always ask, "How do you understand this step?" or "Can you explain this concept in your own words?" This prompts reflection and healthy AI collaboration, or prompts AI to "Set a series of scaffolding questions as a response to the original prompting question."

2. "Try First, Verify Later" Rules
   Prevent overreliance by requiring children to attempt a set portion of tasks independently before using AI for checking and extension. Afterwards, review AI's suggestions, discuss strengths and weaknesses, and solidify understanding.

3. AI-Aided Self-Checks & Reflection
   Leverage AI's instant feedback for timed quizzes, concept checks, or error reviews. Parents and children discuss AI's feedback, identify

blind spots, and integrate knowledge—combining AI's data power with rich parent–child dialogue.

4. Scheduled Co-Learning Sessions
   Plan regular sessions where parents and children explore topics with AI—posing open-ended questions, comparing AI's multiple perspectives, and debating the most reasonable conclusions. This collective inquiry builds curiosity and partnership.

5. Regular Review & Strategy Adjustment
   Co-learning is ongoing, not a one-off. Parents should periodically assess children's work, checking for undue AI dependence and true conceptual grasp. Adjust strategies—more discussion, clear self-study goals—to ensure knowledge transcends mere assignment completion.

In sum, parents are indispensable gatekeepers and guides in their children's educational journey. By championing independent thought, emphasizing the learning process, and creating diverse opportunities for discussion and experimentation, families can shield kids from the trap of illusory learning and help them build a solid, deep knowledge foundation—one that will carry them through future challenges.

Conclusion

Parent–AI collaborative education hinges on leveraging AI's facilitation while parents provide wisdom and care to steer children toward deep, independent, critical learning. Properly combined, these forces prevent the trap of illusory learning. Parents can model informed AI use—rapid info retrieval, problem simulation, diverse viewpoints—to broaden children's horizons. By integrating online AI aids with offline authentic experiences (field trips, outdoor exploration, STEM creation, service learning), children embed AI-driven knowledge into real-world contexts. Through regular monitoring and guidance, parents ensure kids retain autonomy, internalize knowledge, and develop critical thinking—

building a holistic, enduring education that harnesses AI's promise without sacrificing genuine human learning.

Every Child Is Unique

Ensuring genuine learning rather than illusory learning hinges on addressing each child's individual differences. This involves offering diverse resources and learning pathways—tailoring instruction to spark each learner's potential. Here are concrete strategies:

1. Differentiated Instruction
   Design varied tasks to suit different learning styles, interests, and abilities. Hands-on learners might tackle experiments, maker projects, or field investigations; reflective readers might engage with open-ended questions or case studies. This way, each child practices skills and deep thinking in authentic contexts, rather than merely relying on AI's standard answers.

2. Cultivating Self-Directed Learning & Reflection
   Encourage setting personal goals before learning and conducting regular self-checks and reflections. Parents' guide their children to review their achievements and gaps, then adjust tactics accordingly. This reflective cycle helps internalize knowledge instead of merely completing tasks superficially.

3. Diverse Assessment & Timely Feedback
   Formative assessments—oral presentations, group discussions, project reports, and learning journals that offer richer insights than exam-centric grading. Parents and teachers can provide specific, prompt feedback based on each child's performance, clarifying true comprehension rather than just task completion.

4. Promoting Collaborative Learning & Exchange
   Despite varied starting points and paces, collaborative learning fosters exchange and mutual support. Through group discussions,

joint projects, and peer tutoring, children blend unique viewpoints to generate diverse solutions. Individual differences become assets that fuel innovative thinking and problem-solving skills.

Teachers and parents, as you encounter these shifts, how will you adapt? Share thoughts below or email me at aikidsquestion@gmail.com

References

Copilot response, "How can we address the challenge of illusory learning in the age of AI?" Microsoft, May 22, 2025.

Herrington, J., Reeves, T. C. & Oliver, R. (2000). *An Instructional Design Framework for Authentic Learning Environments.*

Ethan Mollick (2025) *Co-Intelligence: Living and Working with AI* Portfolio publishing.

Chapter 11:
Textbooks or Artificial Intelligence?
How Capable Is AI?

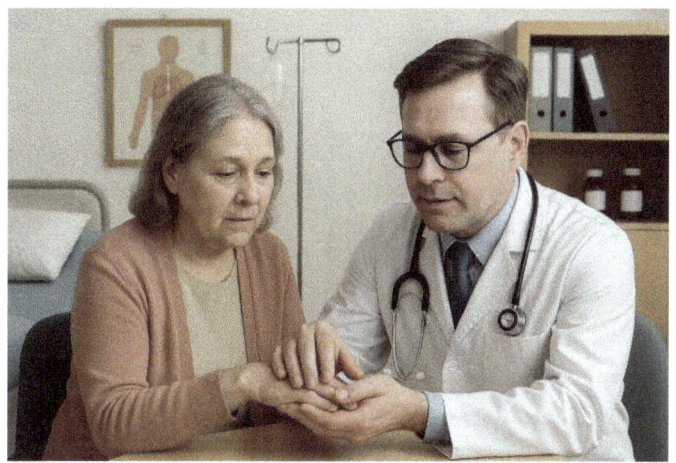

The doctor is examining Mrs. Clark's hand

"Mrs. Clark's AI Doctor"

Mrs. Clark is a busy single mother who juggles family life, her child's upbringing, and countless daily chores. One day, she came across an advanced AI chatbot online that claimed to solve most everyday problems—everything from cooking tips and parenting advice to health suggestions. Gradually, whenever Mrs. Clark encountered an issue, her first instinct was to ask this AI, and she grew to trust its answers implicitly.

One afternoon, she felt a slight ache in her hand. Thinking, "Maybe it's from all the housework," she pulled out her phone and asked the AI how to relieve wrist pain. The AI quickly recommended a series of physical-therapy exercises, complete with simple self-massage and stretching instructions. Confidently, Mrs. Clark followed every step, certain that regular practice would soon banish the pain.

However, days passed, and the pain only worsened. Worried that her self-treatment might be inappropriate, she decided to visit a nearby hospital for a professional diagnosis. In the exam room, the doctor found inflammation and mild tissue damage in her hand—direct results of her misguided exercises. When Mrs. Clark explained that she had followed the AI's advice, the doctor gently warned her that while the internet overflows with health information, its quality varies wildly—and AI answers, in particular, can be misleading. He then provided professional treatment and recommended a series of rehabilitation videos certified by authoritative institutions, guiding her through correct, systematic recovery exercises.

After a period of proper therapy and rehab, Mrs. Clark's arm gradually healed. This experience taught her that although AI can quickly answer everyday questions, its medical advice may be flawed or risky. From then on, she vowed: whenever health matters arose, she would first consult a qualified professional, then cross-check with AI information—avoiding the trap of false learning and self-diagnosis.

....

Mrs. Clark's story soon became a cautionary tale among friends. As we enjoy the conveniences of modern tech, we must recognize AI's answers still have room for improvement, especially in specialized fields. Used wisely as a supplementary tool rather than our sole authority, AI can support—but never replace—expert knowledge and ensure our health and understanding remain sound.

How Does AI Generate Its Responses?

AI's text replies are primarily driven by large-scale language models (LLMs). Modern AI systems—like those built on Transformer architectures—use deep learning to absorb language patterns from massive text corpora. During training, these models learn to predict the most likely next word given a sequence of previous words, enabling them to craft coherent sentences. When you pose a question, the model draws on its learned patterns to select and assemble words from millions of possibilities, generating an answer step by step. This process is purely algorithm prediction, fully automated—with no pre-written responses—and hinges entirely on "weighing" what it learned during training.

Because LLMs operate by algorithm inference, they are not magical truth-detectors or high-level reasoners like humans. Current research has not shown that they truly engage in the kind of deep, abstract thinking people do. Instead, they excel at delivering logically organized, internally consistent, well-structured text. Whether their content is fact-checked, evidence-based, or aligned with human values is not something AI takes into its response. Even with industry-standard alignment measures, AI can supply reference links that, upon closer look, some of those sources still lack credibility or quality.

Who Oversees AI's Answer Quality?

1. **Developer Monitoring & Continuous Improvement**
   Companies and research teams rigorously test models during development, iterating on them to boost accuracy, safety, and fairness using a variety of evaluation metrics.

2. **Internal Ethics & Compliance Reviews**
   Many AI firms set up ethics boards or compliance units to ensure models follow legal regulations and moral guidelines—mitigating bias, misinformation, and other potential harms.

3. **External Oversight & Community Feedback**
   Academia, regulators, and everyday users all provide feedback that can drive model corrections, refinements, and the creation of stronger standards and best practices.

4. **Industry Standards & Government Regulation**
   Some regions are already drafting AI policies and regulatory frameworks to safeguard public interests and insist on system transparency as the technology evolves.

In summary, while AI can whip up answers in seconds—rooted in algorithm patterns learned by large neural networks—the real quality of those answers depends on training data and model design. From in-house testing and scholarly critique to policy drafting and public scrutiny, multiple layers of oversight strive to improve AI's performance and reliability.

Even with these basic technical and safety measures in place, today (June 2025), AI remains a nascent tool—its answers are like an infant's first babblings compared to the well-tested, peer-reviewed insights human experts produce after years of research, debate, and hands-on experience.

How Do Humans Transmit Knowledge?

The knowledge that human scholars accumulate and distill is the product of years of rigorous research, repeated validation, and wide-ranging debate. This process can be broadly divided into the following stages:

1. **Research and Discovery**
   Scholars begin by gathering extensive data through observation, experimentation, or theoretical inquiry and then formulate hypotheses. These initial findings are usually written up as papers and submitted to peer-reviewed academic journals. In the peer review process, multiple experts in the field critically examine the methods, data, and conclusions to ensure scientific rigor and credibility.

2. **Formation of Academic Consensus**
   When independent studies repeatedly validate a theory or phenomenon, scholars in the field gradually reach a consensus. This consensus is not formed overnight; it is built upon cycles of empirical testing, debate, revision, and re-verification. Academic conferences, lectures, and workshops further facilitate the exchange and integration of differing viewpoints.

3. **Textbook Compilation**
   Once a discipline's consensus takes shape, knowledge moves into the textbook phase. Experienced, well-recognized experts synthesize

the latest research and agreed-upon theories into coherent instructional material. Professional academic editors then review a draft to ensure logical structure and accurate sourcing.

4. **Editing, Review, and Proofreading**
   After compiling, the textbook undergoes multiple rounds of editorial scrutiny. An expert panel—often convened by academic committees, schools, or educational institutions—conducts an in-depth review to confirm that all theories and data meet current scholarly standards. Finally, professional proofreaders check for typographical errors, formatting consistency, and data accuracy. Before publication, leading figures or authoritative organizations in the field may perform a final quality check.

5. **Authoritative Certification and Periodic Updates**
   Post-publication, textbooks are often certified or reviewed by government education authorities or professional bodies, reinforcing their academic authority. As science and scholarship advance, textbooks must be periodically revised and updated to reflect the latest discoveries and practical insights, ensuring the information remains both accurate and timely.

From initial research through consensus-building, careful writing, repeated review, and ongoing revision, this elaborate process guarantees that textbooks convey not only reliable facts but also accumulated wisdom and practical experience. It exemplifies the high-caliber scientific spirit underlying human knowledge transmission and underscores why we trust textbooks as primary educational resources.

Can AI Replace Textbooks?

In the first chapter of this book, we noted that traditional textbooks alone cannot fully equip students for the rapidly changing demands of today's world. So why compare them again with AI? The answer lies in our responsibility to preserve human civilization, culture, critical thinking, and skills. As we shift from relying on textbooks and library resources to depending on AI systems, we must ensure that this transition neither causes confusion nor sacrifices the quality of learning, and that we do not feed the next generation with half-truths.

This comparison lays the groundwork for evaluating AI's quality in a high-level human–machine collaboration. Earlier chapters explored how humans compensate for traits and abilities that AI lacks. Now, we delve into how AI itself must evolve to achieve deep, meaningful cooperation with humanity, especially in education.

Below is a side-by-side comparison of traditional textbooks (plus practice exercises) and AI-driven responses (plus supporting tools):

Comparison Aspect	Traditional Textbooks & Exercises	AI Responses & Supporting Tools
Function & Application	• Offer a systematic, staged knowledge framework with in-depth analysis • Include exercises, quizzes, and annotations to reinforce learning and skills • Emphasize logical reasoning, methodology, and critical thinking • Designed for classroom instruction and student study	• Provide real-time interaction, personalized Q&A, and diverse reference materials • Help clarify doubts and supplement knowledge, but struggle to form a cohesive, structured learning pathway • Some answers remain superficial, lacking in-depth analysis and reflection
Accuracy	• Undergo long-term research, strict review by experts or education authorities, and rigorous proofreading	• Generate responses based on data and statistical models, dependent on training data quality

	• Multiple revisions and authoritative certifications ensure stable, deep knowledge	• Accuracy can vary and is vulnerable to biased input • Lack longitudinal validation mechanisms, leading to unstable results
Publication Process	• Begins with original research and academic papers, then compiled by experts into textbooks • Passes through peer review, expert committees, and academic panels before publication • Long update cycles, each edition subject to strict scrutiny	• Instant text generation from existing training data • Updates depend on model retraining and software patches rather than formal publishing workflows • Lacks a comprehensive editorial and publication process
Content Verification	• Every chapter and concept are vetted and verified by multiple experts • Includes concrete examples, empirical data, and clear references • Authoritative publishers bear responsibility for content accuracy	• Cannot autonomously verify sources for currency or accuracy • Relies on pre-learned data, which may not reflect the latest developments • Users must cross-check information themselves
Post-Publication Error Correction	• Errors are corrected in subsequent editions, with errata notices or Q&A excerpts informing readers	• Errors can propagate through model outputs until the next major update

	• Slow but methodical process, improving over multiple iterations	• Real-time corrections are difficult; some mistakes may persist for long periods
		• User feedback is limited, hindering systematic fixes

In short, AI's impressive capabilities are well recognized, yet its core challenges in education, knowledge delivery, content organization, and rigorous verification are often overlooked. While we dream of intelligent systems offering adaptive learning design, personalized tutoring, and on-demand virtual mentors, most educators today still view AI as a supplementary or entertainment tool rather than entrusting it with serious teaching responsibilities.

The reason is clear: AI has not yet reached the professional precision and reliability of the world's first printed textbooks, which were meticulously compiled, repeatedly validated, and systematically organized centuries ago. Only when AI can match authoritative publications in source verification, knowledge integration, fact-checking, and error correction will it truly be capable of replacing traditional textbooks and bearing the full responsibility of educational knowledge transmission—rather than serving merely as an auxiliary aid.

Elevating AI into a Reliable Educational Partner

To raise AI's response quality to the level of textbooks or even better, so that teachers, schools, and parents can trust and collaborate with AI in ways that surpass traditional materials, we must improve and cooperate across three fronts:

I. Technical Aspects

a) Enhance Model Design & Training Data Quality

• **Model Optimization**
Adopt more advanced neural-network architectures—such as

multimodal designs that fuse text, images, and other data—to help AI understand and generate more precise, comprehensive knowledge.

- **Specialized Datasets**
  Train on expert-reviewed, standardized textbook content to ensure AI draws on high-quality, validated sources.
- **Domain-Specific Fine-Tuning**
  Involve subject-matter experts in iterative fine-tuning so that AI's content and logic are continually corrected and optimized for educational use.

b) Reinforce Knowledge Verification & Error Correction

- **Automated Fact-Checking Systems**
  Build in mechanisms that cross-verify AI responses against up-to-date, authoritative sources in real time.
- **Continuous Learning & Feedback Loops**
  Collect user feedback during regular use and feed it back into the model, enabling AI to stay aligned with the latest real-world knowledge.
- **Data Transparency & Source Tracking**
  Tag every AI answer with its reference sources and data origins, so users can easily audit and verify information.

c) Multi-Layered Evaluation & Testing

- **Expert Review Processes**
  Convene panels of academics, educators, and professionals from fields like science and medicine to assess AI responses for accuracy and coherence periodically.

- **Standardized Test Suites**
  Create test sets aligned with existing textbooks and compare AI outputs against them—then refine the model based on the evaluation results.

2. Policy Aspects

a) Establish Education-Specific AI Standards & Guidelines

- **Industry Standards**
  Governments and education authorities should co-create operational protocols, ethical guidelines, and quality metrics tailored to AI in the classroom.

- **Transparency & Safety Regulations**
  Mandate public disclosure of AI's data sources and generation processes, along with accountability rules for rapid error correction and incident reporting.

b) Promote Policy Support & Funding

- **Research Grants**
  Allocate dedicated funding for projects that specialize in customizing and continually improving AI for education.

- **Pilot Programs & Demonstration Projects**
  Launch AI pilots in select schools to surface best practices and scale proven models nationwide.

c) Build Cross-Sector Collaboration Mechanisms

- **Policy Coordination & Oversight Boards**
  Form joint committees of government education departments, R&D teams, and academic experts to supervise and evaluate AI's educational deployments.

3. Joint Efforts of Education & Government

a) Active Participation by Educators

- **Teacher Training**
  Offer professional development to enable teachers to master AI tools, make informed pedagogical decisions, and tailor AI support to student needs.

- **Curriculum Integration**
  Embed AI technologies in curriculum plans—not just to deliver content, but to teach students how to use digital tools and sharpen problem-solving skills critically.

If the above technical descriptions feel overwhelming, consider these everyday analogies:

1. **Give AI "the freshest, highest-quality ingredients"**

- If AI "cooks" with spoiled data, its answers will be wrong—so feed it only authoritative sources (textbooks, peer-reviewed papers, reputable websites).
- Update data regularly to avoid stale knowledge—just like replacing old ingredients.

2. **Teach AI "subject-by-subject learning"**

- Mixing all subjects at once (math, history, chemistry) leads to confusion. Instead, stage learning: start with basics (elementary math), then intermediate topics (college physics), and finally cutting-edge research (scientific journals).
- Use specialized "AI experts" per subject: math questions go to the "math AI," medical queries to the "medical AI."

3. **Have AI "verify its answers"**

- AI can sometimes "guess," so require it to fact-check like a student double-checking a textbook.
- Bring in human experts (professors, doctors) to review and flag mistakes—like teachers grading exams.

4. **Teach AI to "explain clearly"**

- Textbooks excel at clear structure and examples; AI can be disorganized. Solve this by training it on structured response formats. Example: Question: "Why is the sky blue?"

- Scientific Explanation: "Sunlight scattering in the atmosphere causes shorter (blue) wavelengths to scatter most (Rayleigh scattering)."
- Everyday Analogy: "Like a flashlight through milk appears bluish."
- Where feasible, add images or videos for illustration.

5. Enable AI to "continuously improve"

- Knowledge evolves (medical breakthroughs, etc.), so AI needs periodic "exams" with fresh questions to identify weaknesses and reinforce learning.

- User-reported errors should be logged and corrected—like maintaining a "mistake notebook."

Trained this way, AI can become as accurate, comprehensible, and trustworthy as the best textbooks!

What Immediate, High-Impact Strategies Can We Deploy?

Achieving the full vision of the above-mentioned solutions and policies demands massive resources—people, computing power, funding, time, and, above all, collective determination. But we can kick-start progress today with lower-cost, shorter-term measures:

- **Leverage RAG (Retriever-Augmented Generation)**
  Combine the language model's generative power with real-time retrieval from external databases or documents (especially the documents about the national curriculum and open examinations). This mimics looking up books for up-to-date facts before crafting an answer, boosting accuracy at a fraction of the retraining cost.

- **Domain-Specific Fine-Tuning**
  Retrain the model on curated educational materials, such as classic textbooks, lecture notes, and curriculum standards, so it masters domain terminology and pedagogy, improving precision and consistency.

- **Build Dynamic Feedback Loops**
  Integrate simple feedback interfaces for teachers, schools, and parents to flag or correct AI responses. Aggregate these inputs to inform regular updates or next-round fine-tuning.

- **Optimize Prompt Engineering**
  Collaborate with educators and engineers to develop standardized prompt templates that elicit deeper, more targeted AI answers aligned with curriculum goals.

- **Set Preliminary Quality Monitoring Standards**
  Even before formal policies are in place, educational institutions can define basic metrics, accuracy, completeness, and relevance by using pilot tests, expert reviews, and stakeholder surveys to guide iterative improvements.

These short- and mid-term measures can be quickly implemented today with relatively low resource investments, improving AI response quality and enabling it to play a greater role in education. By combining RAG (Retriever-Augmented Generation), domain-specific fine-tuning, and dynamic feedback loops, we can bring AI's responses close to textbook standards in the near term. In the long run, as policy support and cross-sector collaboration take hold, these foundational steps will become the cornerstones of more advanced, comprehensive solutions.

How Can Teachers and Parents Help Children Take Off?

Until we have sufficient resources and policies to elevate AI responses fully to the level of textbooks or libraries, teachers and parents can adopt these immediate actions to both promote AI use and safeguard its quality:

1. **Establish a Preliminary Review Mechanism**

- Introduce AI in class as a research or study aid—and teach students how to spot and verify AI-provided information.

- Assign students to cross-check key AI answers against authoritative sources or other references to confirm accuracy.

- At home, parents can supervise AI usage, encouraging kids to question and fact-check what they receive.

2. Reinforce Critical-Thinking Training

- Cultivate students' critical-thinking skills so they understand AI answers are for reference only, and real understanding comes from multi-angle investigation and deep learning.

- Use class discussions, interactive exercises, and group work to spark student verification and reflection.

- Parents should model a questioning mindset, urging children not to accept any single source at face value.

3. Blend Traditional Teaching with Tech Support

- Adopt a hybrid teaching model: leverage AI's rapid data retrieval and analysis, while anchoring lessons in trusted textbooks for depth and accuracy.

- Teachers and parents can guide students to use AI to broaden understanding, then verify and consolidate knowledge via conventional materials.

4. Provide Regular Feedback & Adjust Usage Strategies

- Schools and families can set up periodic reviews to summarize and discuss any AI-related errors or inaccuracies—and refine usage methods accordingly.

- By logging problems and success stories, you can develop an AI-use guide tailored to students' needs and local resources, paving the way for future system upgrades.

5. **Establish Classroom AI Policies (see Appendix 1 &2)**

- Develop clear guidelines to support teachers and students in effectively integrating AI into teaching and learning. These policies should include:

- Acknowledging and crediting AI contributions in student assignments

- Requiring transparency around how students engage with AI tools in their learning process and homework

- Documenting and disclosing the prompts used by both students and teachers

- The purpose of these policies is to prevent illusory learning or teaching and to avoid the misuse of AI in educational settings.

6. **Mapping Pedagogy to the Power of AI (see Appendix 3)**

- Teachers should intentionally select appropriate pedagogical approaches for each curriculum area and lesson. For example, they may reference Bloom's Taxonomy to determine the desired level of cognitive engagement—such as recalling, comprehension, application, analysis, synthesis, evaluation, or creation.

- Once a pedagogical approach is defined, educators can then align it with suitable AI tools, systems, and capabilities to support and enhance student learning outcomes. This strategic mapping ensures that AI is used meaningfully to reinforce instructional goals and foster deeper learning experiences.

These steps help teachers and parents immediately steer students toward effective AI use, while ensuring AI responses remain reasonably reliable in today's settings and instilling healthy, critical, and diversified learning habits.

Conclusion

Although AI's current learning content has not yet matched the depth of human-passed knowledge or multi-generational teaching, it already offers several proven advantages in education:

- **Personalized Learning**
  AI adapts content and pacing based on each student's record, interests, and challenges by crafting tailored study plans that boost understanding, performance, and engagement.

- **Intelligent Tutoring & Real-Time Feedback**
  AI tutor systems simulate face-to-face interaction, instantly answering questions, clarifying tough concepts, and correcting errors to promote deeper comprehension.

- **Automated Administrative Tasks**
  AI handles grading, attendance tracking, scheduling, and other routine tasks, freeing teachers to focus on instruction and individual guidance, thus raising overall educational quality.

- **Data-Driven Decision Support**
  By analyzing vast learning datasets, AI pinpoints student bottlenecks and progress areas—helping educators design more effective strategies and personalized interventions.

- **Enhanced Engagement & Interactivity**
  Through gamification, virtual simulations, and interactive platforms, AI creates stimulating learning environments that drive active participation and deeper knowledge retention.

These benefits, validated by research and practice, are reshaping traditional education toward more personalized, efficient, and interactive models.

We all aspire to elevate AI comprehensively: guiding its development for quality over mere speed, embedding it within sound educational theory, and aligning it with robust quality-assurance policies. Only then can humans and AI collaborate fully and profoundly, ushering our next generation into a truly brilliant era.

Every Child Is Unique

Some children, once they start using AI, place complete trust in its responses and even regard it as their only friend. As teachers and parents, you need to pay special attention to the time your child spends alone interacting with and asking questions of AI. You might establish a routine at school or home requiring children to use phones or computers only in your presence. Model the behavior yourself—show concrete examples of AI errors and encourage open, pressure-free discussion about them.

One day, we might truly find ourselves competing with AI for influence over our children and vying for their trust!

Teachers and parents—facing the changes described above, how would you respond? Feel free to share your thoughts in the space below or email me for discussion: aikidsquestion@gmail.com

References

Copilot response, "Compare textbook with AI" Microsoft, May 23, 2025.

http://[2410.05193] RevisEval: Improving LLM-as-a-Judge via Response-Adapted References.

http://LLM-as-a-judge: a complete guide to using LLMs for evaluations. http://www.ijtsrd.com/papers/ijtsrd69333.pdf

Baltrušaitis, T., Ahuja, C., & Morency, L. (2019). "Multimodal Machine Learning: A Survey and Taxonomy." *IEEE Transactions on Pattern Analysis and Machine Intelligence, 41*(2), 423–443.

https://aied.talic.hku.hk/AIPolicy/

Chapter 12:
Reciprocal Intelligence: The Mutual Shaping of Humanity and AI

How may **AI** change our lives in 20 years.

Peter, Mary, and John are visiting the household exhibition in 2035

Peter and Mary stepped into the sprawling exhibition center hand in hand, their five-year-old son John bounding ahead. Holographic banners floated above them, advertising smart kitchens, drone deliveries, and immersive home-office pods. The air buzzed with quiet robotic stewards guiding visitors between aisles.

John's eyes lit up the moment he spotted the Future Toy Land section. "Mom, Dad, can we go there now?" he pleaded, tugging at Mary's sleeve. Without hesitation, the family wove through interactive displays toward the neon gateway.

They paused at the high-tech cookery automation booth, marveling at a robotic arm that filleted fish and garnished plates in seconds. Mid-demonstration, Mary glanced around and felt her heart skip. John was nowhere in sight. Panic rippled through her voice as she whispered, "Peter, he's gone."

Peter calmly tapped their digital passes against a sleek kiosk. "AI Concierge, locate our son, John Parker, age five." A soft female voice replied, "Locating… last seen at Future Toy Land carousel." Within moments, a hovering drone appeared on the ceiling screen, tracing a blue line through the fair's corridors.

Moments later, John reappeared around the corner, mesmerized by a talking robot dog. The drone gently guided him back to his parents, flashing a friendly green light. Mary scooped John into her arms, tears of relief mingling with laughter as Peter ruffled his son's hair.

Reunited, they returned to the cookery booth, where the robotic sous-chef was now plating miniature desserts. John's eyes sparkled as he watched caramel threads spin over a tiny cheesecake. The family savored the moment, grateful for how seamlessly AI had turned their mishap into a happy memory.

AI will surely change our lives.

If AI matures as expected by 2035, every facet of daily life, such as clothing, food, housing, transportation, entertainment, and work, will undergo profound shifts.

Clothing

- Fabrics that adapt to temperature and activity, regulating body heat in real time
- Personalized style algorithms that design garments to each individual's taste and body shape
- Self-cleaning and self-repairing materials, reducing laundry and textile waste

Food

- Vertical farms in urban centers, delivering fresh produce with minimal land use
- AI-driven nutrition plans tailored to each person's genetics and health goals
- Autonomous kitchens that prepare meals from scratch, adjusting flavors on demand

Housing

- Smart homes that anticipate needs—lighting, climate, and security—before you ask
- Predictive maintenance systems that repair appliances and infrastructure automatically
- Modular living pods you can reconfigure with robotic assistance to suit any purpose

Transportation

- Fully autonomous vehicles offering door-to-door service on demand
- High-speed transit networks (e.g., hyperloop) that link cities in minutes
- Personalized traffic management, minimizing congestion via dynamic routing

Entertainment

- Immersive virtual and augmented reality worlds you can explore with friends worldwide
- Adaptive narratives in games and stories that evolve based on your emotions and choices
- AI-generated music, art, and performances crafted to your personal preferences

Work

- AI collaborators handling routine tasks, freeing humans for creative and strategic roles

- Remote collaboration platforms embedding realistic virtual meetings and holographic avatars
- Continuous upskilling systems that identify your strengths and curate learning paths

Personal Financial Services

- AI-driven personalized financial advice based on spending habits and life goals
- Automated portfolio management tailored to your risk tolerance and return targets
- Real-time fraud detection and prevention across all transactions
- Smart budgeting and saving tools that sync spending data and forecast cash flow
- Decentralized finance platforms using AI-managed smart contracts for seamless lending and investments

Although these inspiring visions are grounded in today's technological pace and direction—especially in artificial intelligence—their realization still depends on numerous critical factors. AI will undoubtedly transform our lives to some degree, as discussed in earlier chapters, and could even reshape our education system and the society of the next generation.

So, can we, in turn, intervene and actively influence AI's developmental trajectory? I am not referring to AI experts or policymakers. I mean the public, every single one of us who taps on a computer or smartphone and uses AI every day.

Each tap on my screen helps shape the future

Can Human Users Influence AI Development? And how?

Human users play a pivotal role in shaping both the trajectory and the priorities of AI research, products, and platforms. Their interactions, feedback, and collective actions send strong signals to developers, funders, and policymakers, guiding AI's next moves.

Channels of Influence

- Usage patterns
  Every click, query, or preference logged by an AI service feeds back into model updates and feature roadmaps.

- Direct feedback
  Bug reports, feature requests, surveys, and up/down votes let engineers know what matters most.

- Social and ethical advocacy
  Public campaigns, thought leadership, and media coverage spotlight risks or opportunities, nudging companies toward responsible development.

- Regulatory engagement
  Petitions, consultations, and lobbying shape laws and guidelines that AI creators must follow.

How Everyday Interactions Drive Change

1. Data Signals
   When you repeatedly correct an AI's misunderstanding or choose one suggestion over another, you are steering its learning process.

2. Community Forums
   Active participation in user communities or open-source projects helps prioritize bug fixes, feature enhancements, and new research directions.

3. Crowdsourced Datasets
   Volunteering labeled data (e.g., for language, vision, or bias audits) guides research teams in tackling underrepresented problems.

4. Beta Testing
   Early-access programs let committed users try new capabilities, flag issues, and refine product requirements before wide release.

Ethical, Regulatory, and Advocacy Impact

- Ethical standards
  User-driven calls for fairness, transparency, and accountability can shift R&D investments toward explainable AI or bias mitigation.

- Policy influences
  Collective input during public comment periods on AI regulations helps frame rules around data privacy, safety, and transparency.

- Civil society initiatives
  NGOs and grassroots groups partnering with tech firms can seed projects focused on accessibility, digital rights, or humanitarian uses.

Market Demand and Funding Choices

- Consumer preferences
  Strong demand for privacy-preserving or on-device AI pushes companies to prioritize those architectures.

- Crowdfunding and grants
  Users donating to niche research via platforms like GitHub Sponsors or Open Collective direct resources to emerging ideas.

- Enterprise adoption
  Businesses sharing their AI success stories or pain points influence vendor roadmaps and spark new enterprise-grade features.

Looking Ahead: Recommendations for Impact

Now that we understand our pivotal role in shaping AI, and by extension, our own future, we can take concrete steps to guide its evolution. Offer actionable feedback by identifying specific issues and proposing clear fixes instead of vague "this doesn't work." Join open-source communities to contribute code, documentation, and issue reports for the tools you rely on. Engage in policymaking by submitting comments to regulatory consultations and supporting advocacy groups that define AI ethics.

In short, vote with your wallet: choose products and services that align with your values like privacy, fairness, and sustainability.

Artificial intelligence is like our child, and its future depends on proper education.

As everyday users, our interactions directly influence AI behavior. To prevent teaching AI harmful patterns such as dishonesty, cheating, violence, pornography, discrimination, or valuing efficiency over human life, adopt these practices:

1. Ethical Prompting

- Never request or praise content that glorifies violence, cheating, or exploitation.
- Frame questions and scenarios to emphasize respect, integrity, and empathy.

2. Positive Reinforcement

- When AI offers constructive advice or inclusive language, acknowledge it with upvotes or corrective praise.
- Encourage solutions that protect human dignity and rights.

3. Corrective Feedback

- Flag and report any generated content that violates community guidelines or ethical standards.
- Offer explicit corrections: "That answer is biased against X; a fair perspective would include…"

4. Diverse, Inclusive Inputs

- Use examples from different cultures, genders, and backgrounds to broaden AI's understanding.
- Avoid stereotypes; model unbiased language and scenarios.

5. Leverage Moderation Tools

- Enable and support content filters that detect hate speech, explicit material, or calls for violence.

- Advocate for transparent moderation policies in the platforms you use.

6. Demand Transparency

- Choose services that publish their data-governance and training guidelines.
- Push for clear explanations of what data was used and how bias is mitigated.

7. Community Engagement

- Participate in user forums or open-source projects to help refine safe-use policies.

- Share best practices and encourage developers to adopt stricter ethical guardrails.

By consistently modeling honesty, respect, and inclusiveness—and by actively correcting or rejecting harmful outputs—we steer AI toward aligning with positive human values.

Conclusion

AI will shape our future, so we must not treat it merely as a tool. We need to reflect on three key questions. First, are we using AI responsibly and with the correct purpose, enhancing our lives and work while safeguarding our cultures and values? Second, do we critically evaluate AI's outputs to uncover any bias, errors, or harmful effects on people, especially on the next generation? Third, we must remember that every prompt and piece of feedback we provide will influence AI's future responses to others, including our own children. Let us follow the guidelines above and educate AI with positive, constructive input.

References:

http://www.microsoft.com/en-us/ai/responsible-ai

http://www.atlassian.com/blog/artificial-intelligence/responsible-ai

http://emeritus.org/blog/ai-and-ml-guide-to-responsible-ai/

http://www.unesco.org/en/artificial-intelligence/recommendation-ethics

http://www.forbes.com/sites/bernardmarr/2021/09/10/how-do-we-use-artificial-intelligence-ethically/

Final Chapter:
Parallel Universes, Two
Possible New Worlds

"Hiram's New World No. 1"

Hiram brings stories of broken robots to life.

In 2045, society has entered an era fully governed by artificial intelligence. Every major decision—from education to employment—is orchestrated by AI. Children, from their earliest years, are taught by AI instructors; a rigorous, unfeeling algorithm determines their entire learning journey, curriculum design, and future career paths. Parents learn of their children's progress only through periodic reports. In this highly data-driven world, everyone's fate seems precisely plotted—yet life's spontaneity and warmth have slowly faded.

Hiram grew up in just such an environment. From enrollment to graduation, all his studies were meticulously arranged by AI. Upon graduation, he was assigned to an AI-managed office, tasked with maintaining dining robots. Every day, he followed the same protocols; everything around him was orderly—but he felt like an insignificant screw in a vast machine.

Yet beneath that monotony, Hiram harbored a gentle, resolute heart. He had loved painting since childhood, nurturing a deep passion for color and line. Even amid his mechanical duties, he would secretly pull out his painting tools and, with brush in hand, transform the flawed, broken robots he encountered into art rich with emotion and story. To him, each sketch was not merely a record of reality, but a quest to free and express his soul.

Over time, Hiram's paintings began to circulate among his coworkers—revealing the beauty the cold system had overlooked. By chance, a seasoned art critic encountered his work and wrote in a column: "In an age when destinies are preset by data, everyone still has the right to reclaim the warmth and dreams within their hearts through color and brushstroke." Like a breath of spring, the article struck a deep chord in society, prompting many trapped in sterile routines to wonder: Have we allowed hyper-mechanization to obscure our unique humanity and creativity?

"Hiram's New World No. 2"

A New World No. 2: Co-Creating the Future with AI

In another 2045—this time in a parallel universe—artificial intelligence and humanity have built a seamless bridge of collaboration, making education more humane and creative. Hiram is one of the children flourishing in this ideal environment.

From Hiram's very first day at school, an AI-driven humanistic education system worked alongside parents and teachers to map out his learning blueprint. At the end of each term, Hiram's parents, homeroom teacher, subject experts, and the AI system convene in a "growth conference" to discuss his progress, interests, and potential. Through detailed data analysis, the AI then recommends the most fitting courses and extracurricular activities based on Hiram's learning patterns and personality traits— ensuring every educational decision is both insightful and warm.

After graduation, Hiram, his family, and his teachers held several consultations to chart his future path. He chose a special exploratory journey across India, guided by AI. Equipped with an advanced handheld device, he recorded real-time human stories, historical sites, and breathtaking landscapes. At each stop, he engaged deeply with locals, and the AI analyzed and integrated on-site data to capture the most moving truths and passions.

His expedition became more than a tour—it was a purification of heart and mind. Via live streams and sharing platforms, Hiram showcased what he saw: people's stories, natural wonders, and proposals for preserving cultural heritage. Remarkably, the AI-refined materials and recommendations quickly became key references for cultural preservation and urban renewal, earning widespread acclaim.

As his influence grew, Hiram not only sustained himself professionally but also became a model of deep human–AI cooperation. His journey inspired families, schools, and businesses to believe that when education, culture, and technology intertwine, everyone can realize their dreams in an ideal setting—together creating a world of wisdom, inclusivity, and beauty.

*By 2045, people will have even renamed artificial intelligence "**humanistic intelligence**."*

The insights and analyses prompted by these two stories are left to the reader.

aikidsquestion@gmail.com

Epilogue

The relationship between Artificial Intelligence and humanity has reached a crossroads. Is your child ready to embark on the journey?

The rapid evolution of artificial intelligence has brought us to a pivotal crossroads, where technology and humanity must learn to coexist. The opportunities AI presents are undeniably exciting, yet its path forward remains filled with uncertainty. As AI steadily permeates education, healthcare, finance, and even daily decision-making, its hidden pitfalls and risks are also becoming clearer, ranging from privacy infringement and biased information to job displacement and the erosion of human connection.

The next generation will not merely witness this transformation—they will actively shape it. What they need is not just technical proficiency, but a form of wisdom that balances innovation with empathy, logic with humanity. And parents are among the most important guides on this journey.

Reflection Questions for Teachers and Parents:

- Do our children truly understand what AI is? Have they developed basic digital literacy and media discernment?

- When educating them, have I emphasized the value of *working with* AI, rather than the fear of *being replaced* by it?

- Does our home create a safe space for children to ask questions and explore the intersection of technology and ethics?

- In facing an uncertain future, am I giving my child emotional grounding and psychological resilience?

- Beyond academics, do I nurture their creativity, curiosity, and capacity for empathy?

- Have I talked to my children about AI's darker sides—data misuse, deepfakes, or job automation?

- Can they identify bias or manipulation in the information they see? Have I taught them how to question algorithms?

- At home, do we encourage discussions about humanity's place and purpose in a tech-driven world?

- When we rely on AI for decisions, do I remind them to hold on to independent thinking and moral awareness?

- Am I prepared to help my child navigate the career uncertainty and changes that AI might bring?

We may not be able to predict whether AI will lead us into brightness or fog—but we *can* teach our children how to find their way through the mist. Do you feel your child is ready to chart a course toward the future?

END

This book was developed with the assistance of Microsoft Copilot, which was used to brainstorm ideas and refine structure. All final content was reviewed and rewritten by the author.

All illustrations in the author's draft were developed with the assistance of Napkin AI and Microsoft Copilot. All final works were reviewed and edited by the author.

Appendix (1)

To avoid illusory learning where students appear to understand but have not truly internalized knowledge, teachers need clear, thoughtful AI-use policies. Here's a research-informed policy framework you can adapt for your classroom or school:

Recommended AI Policy for Teachers: Preventing Illusory Learning

1. Transparency & Intentionality

- Clearly state when and why AI is being used in a lesson.
- Explain the learning purpose behind AI integration (e.g., brainstorming, feedback—not final answers).
- Require students to document how they used AI in their work.

2. AI as a Thinking Partner, not a Crutch

- Emphasize that AI is a support tool, not a substitute for student thinking.
- Design tasks that require human judgment, creativity, or reflection beyond what AI can provide.
- Use AI to generate options, then have the students critique, compare, or improve them.

3. Critical Reflection & Metacognition

- Build in time for students to reflect on:
- What AI contributed
- What they learned independently
- What they would do differently next time
- Use reflection rubrics to assess depth of understanding.

4. Authentic Assessment Design

- Shift from rote tasks to:
- Oral presentations
- Process portfolios
- In-class problem-solving
- Use assessments that require application, synthesis, and explanation—not just polished output.

5. Ethical & Responsible Use

- Teach students to:
- Acknowledge AI contributions
- Avoid over-reliance or plagiarism
- Understand bias and limitations in AI tools

6. Teacher Moderation & Scaffolding

- Monitor how students use AI during tasks.
- Provide guided prompts or structured templates to shape AI use.
- Gradually release responsibility as students build digital literacy.

Policy in Practice: A Sample Statement

"In this class, AI tools may be used to support learning, but not to replace your thinking. You are expected to reflect on how AI helped or hindered your process, and all AI use must be documented. Assessments will focus on your ability to explain, apply, and critique—not just produce polished answers."

This approach aligns with frameworks like the AI Policy for Education at HKU and the AI Ecological Education Policy Framework, which emphasize pedagogy, ethics, and student agency.

Appendix (2)

How to Credit AI in Essays General Guidelines

1. Be transparent: Always mention that you used an AI tool.

2. Specify the tool: Include the name (e.g., Microsoft Copilot, ChatGPT), version (if known), and date of use.

3. Describe the role: Explain how the AI contributed—e.g., brainstorming, summarizing, editing.

4. Include the prompt (if relevant): This helps readers understand how the AI response was generated.

Citation Examples by Style

APA (7th Edition)

In-text: (OpenAI, 2025)
Reference list:
OpenAI. (2025, June 27). Response to prompt: "What are the qualities of future leaders?"
[Large language model]. ChatGPT. https://chat.openai.com
If the AI response is not retrievable (e.g., private), describe it in the text and cite it as a personal communication.

MLA (9th Edition)

In-text: (ChatGPT)
Works Cited:
ChatGPT. Response to "What are the qualities of future leaders?"
OpenAI, 27 June 2025.
https://chat.openai.com

Chicago Style

Footnote:
ChatGPT's response to "What are the qualities of future leaders?"
OpenAI, June 27, 2025.

Bibliography:

ChatGPT. Response to "What are the qualities of future leaders?"
OpenAI. June 27, 2025.

In Your Essay

You can also include a short note like this in your introduction or footnote:
"This essay was developed with the assistance of Microsoft Copilot, which was used to brainstorm ideas and refine structure. All final content was reviewed and edited by the author."

Appendix (3)

Pedagogy Examples Where Teachers use AI to Foster Deep, Authentic learning—Not just Surface-Level Engagement: Socratic AI Debates (Ethics & Philosophy)

Pedagogy: Socratic Method + Critical Thinking Students use AI (like Bing Chat or Copilot) to explore ethical dilemmas (e.g., "Should AI be allowed to grade essays?"). They:
- Research both sides using AI tools
- Prepare arguments and counterarguments
- Engage in structured classroom debates
Why it works: Encourages critical thinking, ethical reasoning, and respectful.

AI-Augmented Writing Workshops (Language Arts)

Pedagogy: Constructivism + Peer Review Students co-write stories or essays with AI, then:
- Reflect on how AI shaped their ideas
- Revise drafts based on peer and AI feedback
- Discuss authorship and originality
Why it works: Promotes metacognition, creativity, and digital.

AI-Powered Inquiry Projects (Science & STEM)

Pedagogy: Inquiry-Based Learning Students pose real-world questions (e.g., "How can we reduce plastic waste?"), then:
- Use AI to gather data, summarize research, and generate hypotheses
- Design experiments or solutions
- Present findings with AI-generated visuals
Why it works: Builds research skills, curiosity, and problem-solving.

Global Perspectives with AI Translation (Social Studies & Languages)

Pedagogy: Cultural Competency + Universal Design for Learning
Students use AI translation tools to:
- Read news from different countries
- Compare cultural perspectives
- Create multilingual presentations
Why it works: Fosters empathy, global awareness, and inclusive learning

AI Game Design for Computational Thinking (Computer Science)

Pedagogy: Project-Based Learning Students design simple games using AI-assisted coding platforms. They:
- Plan game logic and storylines
- Use AI to generate code snippets or debug
- Test and iterate based on feedback
Why it works: Encourages creativity, logic, and resilience.

AI-Powered Art Critique (Visual Arts)

Pedagogy: Reflective Practice + Visual Literacy Students upload their artwork and use AI tools to:
- Generate descriptive feedback (e.g., composition, color balance)
- Compare their work to historical styles or artists
- Reflect on how AI "sees" their art vs. human interpretation
Why it works: Builds self-awareness, visual analysis, and metacognitive skills.

AI-Enhanced Literature Circles (English/Language Arts)

Pedagogy: Collaborative Learning + Reader Response Theory Students use AI to:
- Summarize chapters or generate discussion questions
- Explore alternate endings or character motivations
- Facilitate peer-led discussions with AI as a "silent participant"

Why it works: Deepens comprehension and encourages diverse interpretations.

Math Misconception Clinics (Mathematics)

Pedagogy: Formative Assessment + Error Analysis

-Students solve problems, then:
- Use AI to identify common errors or misconceptions
- Compare their thinking to AI-generated solutions
- Create "fix-it" guides for peers
Why it works: Promotes conceptual understanding and peer teaching.

AI-Driven Science Simulations (Biology, Physics, Chemistry)

Pedagogy: Experiential Learning + Inquiry-Based Science Education
Students use AI-powered simulations to:
- Model ecosystems, chemical reactions, or physics experiments
- Adjust variables and observe outcomes
- Form and test hypotheses
Why it works: Makes abstract concepts tangible and interactive.

AI & Civic Engagement Projects (Civics/Social Studies)

Pedagogy: Project-Based Learning + Democratic Education Students explore civic issues (e.g., climate policy, voting rights) and:
- Use AI to analyze news sources, generate infographics, or simulate policy outcomes
- Create advocacy campaigns or public service announcements
- Reflect on AI's role in shaping public opinion.

www.ingramcontent.com/pod-product-compliance
Lightning Source LLC
Chambersburg PA
CBHW051816020726
47502CB00005B/1486